BROKEN BROTHERHOOD

An Outlaw Biker Tale

Alex McRae

Published by Iron Battalion Press

Made in the USA

2025

Visit Alex McRae at www.alexmcrae.net to sign up to the author's newsletter and learn more about Iron Battalion books.

Twitter : @AlexMcRae99

"Our brotherhood is what ensures our survival and preserves our way of life. What truly matters is the courage in your heart and the bond you share with your brothers."

CONTENTS

CHAPTER ONE

Biker Johnny "Ace" McIntire got up to take a piss. What was that now, the third time tonight? Fuck, he loved drinking beer, always had. But in recent years, he found that whenever he went out drinking, he spent half the night waking up, taking a piss and going back to bed. It was never like that in the old days. He could drink all night, pass out, wake up the next day and what do you know? He was good to go. He first recalled this happening about ten years ago, but it had gotten worse in recent years. Sometimes, even when he didn't drink beer, he had to get up in the night to piss. Getting old sucked. His knees were shot, his right hip. Hell, don't get him started on his right hip; he knew sooner or later he would have to get a hip replacement. But just how the hell could he pay for that?

Johnny always prided himself on his excellent eyesight but in the last few years he had resorted to carrying around reading glasses. He could see most things but if he was ever eating out and the restaurant had poor lighting, he struggled to read the amount to pay for the check. He was just glad he didn't need prescription glasses to ride. At least he still had his sight for riding. Speaking of declining faculties, his hearing was shot too.

He used to laugh at guys who had to put earplugs in before they rode, but now he wished he had done the same. There were nights where he lay in bed trying to fall back to sleep and both his ears had a dull ringing from years of riding Harleys. Oh well, what was the saying? Hindsight is 20/20. If he knew then what he knew now, would he have done anything differently?

He flushed and went back to bed. How much more sleep would he get before he had to get up and piss again? He hoped for at least another hour. Times like this led to exhausting days at work the next day with a night of broken sleep. It sucked, but he had resigned himself to it. He had no intention of ever stopping his beer drinking, so he had just learned to live with it.

Johnny's alarm went off at 4:30 a.m. He could have done with more sleep but hey, that's what you get for going out drinking mid-week. Johnny was assistant foreman on a big construction site on Camelback, one of these commercial buildings being converted into high-end apartment buildings. He once had his own electrician's business, back when he lived in Tucson, but sold it when his first wife took the kids and fled to Phoenix because he wanted to remain in their lives. He had tried to start again in the Phoenix metro area but kept hitting so many obstacles. After that, he found it easier to work for someone else. Just turn up, do your job and collect your paycheck. No dealing with tax accountants, payroll and ungrateful, unruly employees.

His back pinged as he got out of bed. He could lift a downed 600-pound motorcycle without issue but getting out of bed and turning ever so slightly nearly crippled him. How did that make any sense? He figured years of riding hard-tail choppers had destroyed his spine. Oh well, definitely no regrets there. If he could afford it, he would hit the chiropractor twice a month to keep his spine flexible.

Somehow, he made it through his day by pounding coffee to stay awake. No energy drinks for him; they always made him feel like his heart was going to explode. Of course, after wanting to sleep all day long, by the time he got home from work he was wide awake. Isn't that always the way?

He sat on his lazy boy after dinner flicking through the TV channels to try and find something that held his interest. Over 100 channels and most of them sucked ass. How much did he pay for all the streaming services these days? Probably more than his old Cable TV package and there was less cool stuff to watch. He eventually found a re-run of an old cop show from the '80s and settled on that.

His phone beeped and he reached over and grabbed it. It was his best friend in the world, Joe "Moose" Murdock. The two of them had been club brothers back in the day and were still friends even after sharing 100,000s of road miles together. A true sign of real brotherhood. Johnny had seen best friends throw down on the side of the road

3

hundreds of miles from anywhere over the most trivial things, like the way someone eats a bag of potato chips over the years, but he and Joe were always solid.

Joe's text simply said, "Beers tomorrow night?"

Johnny smiled to himself. Despite all the aggravations drinking beer caused him these days, he would never say no.

"Sure," he replied. "The Filthy Hogg saloon, 7 p.m.?"

Moments later his phone beeped again. The sure sound of a new text message. It was Joe's reply.

"Cool, see ya then."

Fuck it, thought Johnny, *at least I can sleep in Saturday.*

Friday night beers were on!

CHAPTER TWO

Johnny breezed through work on Friday. Funny how much easier working was after a proper night of sleep with no frequent trips to the bathroom. After work he came home, showered, had a quick bite to eat and grabbed his bike for the ride out to the Filthy Hogg bar on Cave Creek Rd. On the ride in Johnny reflected how much his taste in bars changed as he got older. In his club days he preferred bars with ear-splitting loud rock music and a gaggle of hot girls in attendance. Even if you had no plans to hit on them, the view was still well worth it.

These days he just wanted a quiet bar where he could sit and talk to his friends without having to worry about backing up your club brothers in a bar brawl with some drunken idiots. Okay, well, to be fair, he had to admit in his wild and crazy twenties it was probably him starting the fights with the drunken idiots. He was too old for that crap these days.

Johnny parked his Harley next to the long row of bikes and entered the establishment. He looked around for Joe but couldn't spot him, so he grabbed a PBR and a shot of whiskey and headed to the back patio to avoid the jukebox playing inside. It was still hot in Phoenix (permanent summer), but it was cool enough to sit out back without needing air conditioning. Joe was usually a few minutes late but never kept him waiting too long.

He sent a quick text, "Here, outside on patio," and kicked back to enjoy his well-earned beer.

CHAPTER THREE

Joe "Moose" Murdock weaved through traffic on the 202 Freeway on his way to meet his brother Johnny. Well, they were not real brothers but had been riding bikes together for over forty years, so in that respect they were probably closer than most brothers.

When Johnny's first marriage had fallen apart and he sold everything to move out to Phoenix to be closer to his kids, Joe didn't hesitate and followed him up. When Johnny had first started hanging around the infamous Steel Reapers Motorcycle Club, Joe followed suit. When Johnny started prospecting for the Reapers, so did Joe. Heck, they both made full patch on the same day. When Johnny finally hung up his patch and was out good with the club, Joe notified the club he was out too. He would never admit it, but Johnny was like the older brother he never had growing up.

Lane splitting was kind of a gray area in Arizona. Technically it was legal in stopped traffic but not in free-flowing traffic. For this reason, Joe stuck to the carpool lane where possible and kept his lane splitting down to a last resort on the Arizona highways. Besides, California commuters were used to riders splitting lanes; Arizona drivers not as much. All it took was tearing up at sixty miles per hour between two lanes of cars and some jackass pulling out and boom, you were going to have a bad day. Joe saw the exit ramp for the 51 freeway north and had to cut over four lanes to make his exit.

As Joe headed north on the 51, traffic started to thin out. He heard his phone go and he knew instinctively it would be Johnny. Chances were he was either letting Joe know he was running late for the bar or already there, take your pick. Either was fine for Joe. He liked the Filthy Hogg despite it being a good thirty to forty minute ride from his home in suburban Chandler. He could simply sit at the bar alone and run into multiple people he knew from his years on the Arizona bike scene.

He was making good time up the 51 and then Joe had to think hard on which exit would take him to Cave Creek Rd. Was it Shea? Nope, the exit for Cactus was the one he needed. Why did he always space on that? Oh well, the main thing was he remembered before it was too late. Sometimes riding his bike he was so "in the moment" he would have a brain fart and forget where he was meant to be going. Riding was like that for him — very Zen.

Joe found the bar on Cave Creek Rd and pulled in. Parking his bike with the row of others he thought he spotted Johnny's scoot in with the other Harleys. Seeing his brother's bike reminded him that his phone had gone off in his pocket on the ride up. He pulled it out of his riding vest and checked his messages. Sure enough, it was from Johnny.

He went inside and hit the bar. After getting his order of two Modelo's and two whiskey shots he made his way to the back yard patio to seek out Johnny. It took him approximately two seconds to spot Johnny in the crowd of bikers and their old ladies.

He laid the drinks down on their table and greeted Johnny. Upon seeing Joe, Johnny got up and gave him a big bear hug.

"Hey brother, great to see ya. How was the ride in?" asked Johnny.

"Great seeing ya too." Joe smiled as he sat down.

"How's tricks bro?" asked Joe.

"Ahhh, I'm good," Johnny explained. "Honestly, eh I'm okay, things could be better. Actually, pretty shit if I say so myself."

"Damn son, what's going on?" asked Joe.

"Ah just life man, can't seem to get ahead," said Johnny. "I'm so far behind on my house repayments if I don't do something soon, I may lose it."

"Whoa, dude wtf, thought you had it all paid off?"

"Well, I paid it off a few years ago but when Amanda left, she wanted half the house, so I had to do a reverse mortgage to pay her off."

"Shit, sucks man," commiserated Joe. "I'm sure you'll figure something out."

Joe raised his shot glass and chinked it against Johnny's whiskey shot.

Johnny grabbed his and returned the gesture. The duo downed their shots and swigged on their beers to chase the brown liquor down.

"Yeah, I hope so," Johnny replied.

The pair drank more beers as the night went on and reminisced about the good old days of running with the Steel Reapers when they were in their twenties.

"You know what I regret?' asked Johnny.

"No, what's that?" Joe replied.

"When Tommy and the boys were importing coke in the '90s, I should have gone in with them."

Joe thought for a moment. The guys in the club who were running drugs back and forth from Mexico had all been caught by an undercover and were sentenced to thirty years a piece prison time for "running a major trafficking ring." *Why would Johnny have wanted to be part of that?*

"Yeah, but they all got serious time bro, don't you remember? Nearly bought the club down," Joe replied.

"Nah nah, you're not getting me. Dave didn't. He made his money, invested in some real businesses and got out before the rat snitched on them all."

"Yeah, but Dave's the exception to the rule, Ace, or did you forget that?" Joe countered.

"Yeah, but that's what I am talking about. You go in, do a few deals, make some big bucks, get out and not get greedy. That's what I should have done," said Johnny.

"Well hindsight is 20/20," Joe replied. "It's not like we have a time machine."

"Yeah, well, I wish we did. A few hundred thousand right now would solve all my problems," Johnny mused. "Pay off the house loan, maybe start my own business."

"I hear ya man, but don't stress it, your luck will change," said Joe, trying to cheer up his club brother.

Johnny got up to go grab them more beers. Joe sat there thinking about money, kind of surprised that Johnny was having such a hard time. Then again, pretty much everyone was having a hard time financially right now.

Johnny returned with two beers and placed them on the bar table, then sat back down.

"You know I saw this documentary on cocaine once," he started.

"Oh yeah?" asked Joe, wondering where this was going.

"Basically, it followed it from the jungles in South America to the cities in the Northeast. At each stop the value increased, from like fifty dollars a kilo in the jungles to hitting 20,000 dollars a key in the USA."

"I think I might have seen that one or something similar," Joe replied.

"Yeah, so even once it arrives in the cites of Mexico it's still super cheap," Johnny continued.

"Yeah, but the real money comes from bringing it over the border, Ace, or are you forgetting that simple fact?" asked Joe. "It's the high risk that puts the cost up."

"True, but if you know someone or let's say a way to cross the border you would be laughing, wouldn't ya?"

"Yeah, I guess," Joe replied. "But I still wouldn't recommend it as a career path, ya know?"

"Well, nah, but it would be a great way to get some quick cash, brother." Johnny shrugged.

"I guess," Joe replied, getting bored with the topic.

The duo sat and finished their beers, talking about the old times before saying their goodbyes and heading to their respective homes.

CHAPTER FOUR

Midweek after work Joe was sitting at home with his feet up chilling when his phone went off. Most people just texted him these days, so he figured it was probably important and took the call. It was Johnny.

"Hello?" he answered.

"Hey man, so that thing we were talking about last weekend," Johnny said without asking how Joe was doing.

'Wait, what thing? We talked a bunch on Friday night," Joe replied.

'You remember, traveling down to Mexico and..."

Suddenly, Joe realized what exactly Johnny was about to say next.

"No, no, not on the phone bro, c'mon now!" Joe admonished Johnny. Had he learned nothing from the feds sting operations of the '90s?

"Ah shit, you're right, want to meet for a beer?" suggested Johnny. "We can talk face to face."

Joe had told himself he wouldn't drink mid-week anymore, but his curiosity was up, and he wanted to hear what Johnny was going on about.

'Sure, what about the Rebel's Roost on Indian School Rd?" Joe figured that was probably about halfway between Johnny's place and his.

"Sure–gimmie thirty minutes," Johnny responded.

"See ya then," Joe said and hung up.

He grabbed his riding gear, gave his bike a once over and then headed over to Indian School Rd to hear out his crazy friend.

CHAPTER FIVE

Joe managed to get there before Johnny and scoped out an outside table where they could talk without people listening in. He grabbed two beers at the bar inside, returned to the outdoor patio and sat down.

Joe was halfway through his first beer when Johnny arrived. He sat down, grabbed his beer and "cheersed," Joe then took a nice long swig of his own.

"Ahh I needed that," he stated.

"So, what's the big emergency?" Joe asked his longtime friend.

"So, check this out," said Johnny, bursting with his news. "A good friend of mine has a ranch right on the border near Nogales."

"Okay…" said Joe, once again wondering where this conversation was going.

"If we ride down there, make a connection, he says we can ride through his property to get back into the country and avoid the border patrol."

Joe was somewhat impressed. What had just been drunk talk last week at the bar, Johnny had turned into the semblance of a plan.

"You're forgetting one thing," Joe added.

"What's that?" asked Johnny.

"We don't have a connect down there."

"I can ask around," said Johnny hopefully.

Just to play along, Joe suggested, "Why don't you ask Old Man Carter–think he still lives south of the border."

"Who?" asked Johnny.

"Hank Carter–you remember him, right?" explained Joe. "He married that big booty Latina who was twenty years younger than him, left the club and moved to Mexico in the early 2000s."

"Oh yeah, the old man." Johnny smiled. "He's still alive?"

"I guess so." Joe shrugged. "Haven't heard anything to the contrary."

"Good thinking. I'll ask around, someone must have his number. Shit, how old was he in 2000?" asked Johnny.

Joe laughed. "You know what, I wanna say mid-fifties. We thought he was soooo old back then. Now we're older than he was."

"Damn, that's crazy," Johnny replied.

"I'll ask some of the boys if they have an email addy or phone number for him, okay?" said Joe, trying to help out.

"Thanks brother, much appreciated," Johnny replied.

The duo finished their beers and said their goodbyes before climbing back on their bikes and heading home. On the ride home, Johnny was glad he had stuck to just two beers. Maybe he would get a good night's sleep tonight. No more midnight bathroom breaks.

CHAPTER SIX

True to his word, Joe came through with a number for the Old Man. Johnny had forgotten about him despite the guy being such a stabilizing influence on him (and Joe) during their wild and crazy twenties with the club. They were young and dumb, yet Hank "Old Man" Carter always tried to steer them right, despite the fact that they felt like he was ruining their fun back then. Because of him, neither Joe nor Johnny did any serious prison time back in the '80s and '90s, nor did they die doing dumb stuff on their bikes like a lot of their friends had back then.

He was a tough old buzzard, tough but fair. He had taught them never to look for trouble but be the first to throw down when trouble found you. He had seen the old man knock out guys two at a time during bar room brawls back in the day. Johnny shuddered to think of trying to have a bar fight these days. Not only did most establishments have security cameras, but ninety-five percent of the patrons would whip out their cell phone and record you. Exhibit A in court, your honor. *Heck, we got away with blue murder back in the '80s,* Johnny reflected.

He dialed the number Joe had supplied him with and let it ring. No one answered–he hated leaving voice messages but left one anyways.

"Hey Hank, this is Johnny, oh you would know me as 'Ace.' We used to ride together in the MC. Call me back," he explained.

He tossed his phone down and started to look for something to watch on TV. Moments later, his phone rang.

"Hello?" he asked.

"Hey, this Johnny?" the voice asked.

"Yeah, that's me. This you, Hank?"

"Hey Johnny, good to hear from ya man. What's it been, twenty years?" Hank asked.

"Yeah, something like that." Johnny smiled to himself. *Fuckin' twenty years. How did that happen?*

"You still with the club?" asked Hank.

"Nah, I was out good a few years back," Johnny explained. "I'll tell ya next time I see ya."

"Oh, you coming down for a visit?" said Hank.

"Yeah possibly, got to ask you something."

"Okay shoot."

"You've been down there a long time. I don't suppose you have any connections..."

'Whoa whoa. Stop right there, brother. Just stop. I'm hanging up now, but I'll text you in ten seconds, okay?"

"Um… okay?' said Johnny, hanging up his cell phone.

Johnny waited–seconds later, his phone pinged, and he checked it. Sure enough, a message from the old man.

"Download the telegram app. Once you have done that text me back using the app. Same number."

Telegram? What's that? Some form of TikTok crap? thought Johnny. He shrugged his shoulders and followed the instructions. After a couple of minutes messing about he had the app installed. Heck, if the old man could figure out apps like this, then he could too.

He texted the old man back and waited. Moments later, his phone rang but the ring tone sounded different. Must be the app, he figured.

"Hello?" he answered.

"Hey brother, it's me," Hank explained.

"Hey," Johnny replied, a little taken aback by the covert skullduggery.

"Look, I know you're good. A solid guy. But I don't trust the feds and tapped phone lines. With Telegram everything is safely encrypted. We can talk freely now."

"Ahh, good thinking brother," Johnny replied.

"Yeah, so what's up?" asked the old man.

"Well, me and Moose want to know if you have any connects for, you know...."

"Moose? Moose? Remind me, what's his real name again? Jeff something?" asked the old man.

"Joe! Joe Murdock," Johnny explained.

"Ah that's right. I knew it began with a J." Hank laughed. "So, let me guess, you need a connect south of the border, right?"

"Pretty much," said Johnny.

"Okay, I could do that for you. What are you looking to buy?" asked Hank.

"Ahh marching powder??" Despite the app being fully encrypted Johnny still felt nervous saying it out loud.

"Yeah, I figured as much, but I meant how much?" Hank explained.

"Oh I see," Johnny replied. "Hmmm I guess a few keys each. Maybe like ten each?"

"Yeah, we could do that," Hank said calmly. "But let me tell you, you will need some extra cash, just to grease the wheels if you get me."

"Sooo, what are we talking about here?" asked Johnny.

"Well, your gas, food, dope money, 'fines and contributions' money. Hmm off the top of my head, I reckon you'll both need 2000 dollars or so," said Hank.

"Okay thanks brother," Johnny responded. "I'll talk with Joe and get back to you in a day or so, okay?"

"Yeah, I'll be around. Good to hear your voice, Johnny," said Hank. "Bye, for now."

"Later Hank," said Johnny, hanging up.

Johnny reflected on their conversation. Well, it was doable by the sound of things, but if he had a spare few thousand dollars why would he need to traffic dope? There had to be a way he could raise the cash.

CHAPTER SEVEN

After work the next day, Johnny called Joe.

"Hey bro, you got time for a quick chat?" he asked his long-time riding buddy.

"Yeah Johnny, what's up?"

"So, I talked to the old man, and he's down to help us."

"Oh shit, so this is really going down?" asked Joe.

"Yeah, certainly seems that way," Johnny replied. "He can put us in touch and help us do the deal and all that, just one problem."

"There's always a catch," Joe remarked. "So, what's the catch?"

"We are going to need some startup money," said Johnny.

"Well, that makes sense. If you want to start any business you need cash first. That's the way of the world," Joe replied. "What are we talking about here?"

"Well, we will need travel money, meaning gas, food hotels etc.," started Johnny.

"Yeah, that makes sense," Joe said.

"Then we will need money to 'grease the wheels' so to speak," added Johnny.

"That makes sense, paying off federales or whatever. I have heard about that," Joe said.

"Then we will need money for the, uh stuff, um you know," said Johnny awkwardly.

"Yeah, I know what you mean," Joe replied. "So, what does that come to?"

"Ahh well, old man Hank reckons about 2000 dollars each all in, but to err on the side of caution I reckon we should aim to bring at least 2500 each with us," explained Johnny.

Joe thought for a moment. "Yeah, I could probably do that," he responded. "And what would be looking to make from this entire escapade?"

"Well, I am doing a quick calculation I reckon we could end up making about 200,000 dollars each."

"Wooowww." Joe whistled. "Not bad for a day's work, eh?"

"Yeah, it's worth it I think," Johnny replied. "And like we said at the bar, this is just a one and done, ya know?"

"Yeah, I agree bro. That's where people get caught. They get greedy and keep going back and forth. Every trip you take ups the odds. One and done ONLY," Joe said.

"Well, here's my problem brother," Johnny replied. "I ain't got 2500 dollars lying around. Shit, if I had that I could pay off some of my mortgage, ya know?"

Joe thought for a minute.

"You would be taking your Street Glide, right?" asked Joe.

"Yeah, duh, of course," said Joe. "Ain't taking my Chopper. It's fine for bar hopping but not long-distance trips. Bro, c'mon, I'm old, my back is trashed. I wouldn't last fifty miles on my Shovel head."

Joe laughed. "Yeah, I figured as much, so there's your solution."

"Huh? I don't get ya. What are you talking about?"

Joe laughed again "C'mon man, sell ya damn Shovel head and use that money to fund the trip."

"Aww shit, I can't sell that bike, that's like selling your first-born child bro, geez," said Johnny.

"You can, and you will!" Joe said sternly. "Besides, if we make as much money as you think we will, you can always buy it back. Heck, you could buy two of them, nah three of them man. Think big brother."

"Dammit Joe, you're right," Johnny replied. "Ugh I hate this but yeah, it's got to be done."

"Maybe try Facebook marketplace, get a cash deal and you won't have to declare your income to the tax man," Joe suggested.

"Okay Joe, I'll try that. Hey, you think you can help out? I have no clue on stuff like that," Johnny replied.

"Sure man, I'll swing by Saturday and walk ya through the process, alright?"

The duo said their goodbyes and hung up.

While Johnny hated the idea of selling his beloved Chopper, he knew it was the fastest way for him to raise the cash for their trip south of the border. Besides, as Joe pointed out, he could always buy it back afterwards — once they were done in Mexico.

CHAPTER EIGHT

With Joe's help Johnny actually managed to sell his Shovel head chopper through Facebook marketplace. After a few kooks had swung by to check out his scoot, he actually met a cool biker who, like Joe and himself, was based in Phoenix. He felt like he was giving his favorite pet away to the animal shelter but as sad as he was to see her go, he knew he had to give her up to get something new. He actually managed to get a 1000 bucks more than he had expected her to sell for, so there was at least that bittersweet victory.

Johnny made one payment to his home loan. Technically he could have paid the entire thing off with the proceeds of his bike sale, but he decided he would pay just enough to keep the bank from reporting his home and would invest the rest in his trip to Mexico with Joe and Hank and come back to the USA a wealthy man. Maybe it wasn't the financially prudent thing to do, but he had lived his entire life doing what people told him not to do, so why stop now?

After Johnny had paid his bank, he called old man Hank on the Telegram app. No reply, so he texted the geezer with a message to call him. A day later Hank finally called him back.

"What's up Ace?" asked the old man.

"Hey brother, thanks for calling me back," said Johnny. "Just wanted to let you know we have our finances sorted out. What's our next step?"

"Ah, that's cool," Hank replied. "Let me ask you a stupid question though."

"Okay, ask away," Johnny replied.

"You both have passports, right? You can't just ride down here with a driver's license anymore," Hank explained.

"Ah shit that's right, I totally forgot they changed the ruling. Thanks for the reminder," Johnny replied. "I definitely have mine, just gotta find it. Not sure on Joe. I will call him after this and confirm."

"Okay great," said Hank. "So when are you thinking of doing this?"

"I've got some holiday time due to me–how does late September sound?"

Hank thought for a moment. "So in like 2 weeks' time?"

"Yeah, if that's okay with you," Johnny said.

"Yeah, should be fine. Let me make some calls and put the wheels in motion," Hank explained.

"Thanks man, this is much appreciated. Just know we will take care of you when this is all said and done."

"I appreciate that Ace, I really do," Hank replied.

"Of course," said Johnny. "So, I will start plotting a route to you. I assume we ride past Tucson and cross into Nogales, yeah?"

"No, no, you are going to need to ride to Las Cruces in New Mexico and cross into Ciudad Juarez, that's where I am," Hank said.

"Ah shit, not sure why I thought you were in Nogales, bro," said Johnny. "How do you spell it? See you da wah rez? Or?"

Hank laughed. "No, no, it's C-i-u-d-a-d J-u-a-r-e-z."

"Ah shit—how did I not know that?" Johnny laughed.

"Have you ever been to Mexico before brother?" asked Hank.

"Yeah, me and the boys had a fun weekend in TJs in the early '90s," Johnny replied.

"Tijuana has changed a lot since then, Ace," Hank explained.

As Hank was talking, Johnny looked at a google map on his computer.

"Hold up, is Seeyoudad Wahrez the same place as Juarez? Isn't that the most dangerous city in the world or something?"

"Geez, some people believe all the media hype," swore Hank "Well, to be honest with ya, when I first moved down here it was pretty rough but no worse than the worst parts of Chicago or Detroit."

"You sure about that bro?" asked Johnny.

"Well. There are still some dangerous areas, but in general, as long as you are not an idiot, you're going to be fine, so just chill man," said Hank.

"I'm chill," reassured Johnny. "Was just asking, that's all."

"Alright, well, find out if Joe has his passport. I guess if he doesn't have one, he is going to have to pay to get it expedited," said Hank. "And then get back to me."

"Sounds like a plan," Johnny responded.

"Hey Johnny," Hank added. "You know what would be super helpful."

"What's that Hank?" asked Johnny.

"If you can Venmo me some startup costs money and I will book us some hotel rooms in advance."

"Ah okay, what are we talking about here?" asked Johnny.

"250? 300 dollars should cover it," Hank explained.

"Looking forward to seeing ya both," said Hank. "I gotta go. Text me if you have any more questions."

"Will do and thanks again Hank," said Johnny before hanging up the call.

CHAPTER NINE

Johnny checked with Joe and sure enough, he still had a passport. *When did he get that? The guy never travelled abroad,* as far as Johnny could remember. Oh well, the main thing was he had it.

The duo spent the next week planning their road trip. According to the old man, they should allow about seven days to make the round trip. Johnny figured the old man would only want to do short runs, but they could probably manage the entire road trip door to door in six days. Joe said they should give it seven days anyways just so they weren't stressed coming home.

The plan was they would both carry backpacks with socks, T-shirts and underwear in them, tool rolls and bedding on their front handlebars and leave their saddle bags empty to bring the goods home. If they needed extra space in their backpacks, they could always toss dirty socks, shirts and boxer shorts out as they travelled as it would only cost a few bucks each to replace once they returned home.

Over beers the boys argued what tools would be the most essential to carry with them. Joe figured gas cans and water would be most essential. Johnny wanted a small five-in-one screwdriver, some wrenches, duct tape and a couple of tire repair kits. He had never been so deep into Mexico, but he imagined there were probably a lot of roads where gas stations were few and far between.

Finally, it was the night before they were due to ride. Joe had stayed over at Johnny's place so they could get an early start, and the duo made sure that they both had their passports, cash and all their essentials. In the morning, it was go time.

Johnny figured it would take them about six to seven hours to get to Las Cruces in New Mexico. Driving it would probably be quicker but with stops for gas and hitting the restroom he figured seven hours should cover it. It had been a few years since either of them had ridden more than three hours in a day so he wanted to ease into the longer runs they would be doing. They hit his favorite breakfast spot for bacon, eggs, hash browns, toast and coffee at 9 a.m. to avoid the breakfast rush and Johnny made sure both he and Joe hit the bathroom before they left just to be sure. At his age, he had a rule that even if you don't think you need the bathroom, hit it anyways before you leave for a road trip. Last thing they needed was a ticket for public urination on the side of a highway in Mexico when they were carrying a bunch of coke on their bikes.

As they left the diner and headed for their bikes, Joe turned to Johnny and asked, "So what's the plan then?"

"It's easy bro," explained Johnny. "We are just gonna jump on the I-10 heading east and hit Las Cruces. If at any time ya gotta piss or pull over, just wave at me, get my attention and give me the fist symbol."

"The fist?" asked Joe.

"Yeah, that's the international sign for stop, or so I have been told," said Johnny. "I guess we should have invested in headsets to talk to each other but too late now. Maybe when we get to see the old man he will have a better system."

"Okay, that works for me," Joe replied. "I just took a piss so I should be good for a couple of hours riding."

"Yeah, me too, however, I gotta warn ya coffee goes right through me so we might have to stop at that rest stop halfway to Tucson."

"Yeah brother, no problem, I know that one," Joe replied. "You all set? Let's get this show on the road."

"Fuck yeah brother, been too long since we did a weeklong road trip together," Johnny said. "I reckon maybe twenty years?"

"I think you're probably right," Joe replied, pulling on his helmet. Even though Arizona was a no helmet law state, they were not sure on New Mexico or Mexico itself so they figured it best to bring em. Besides, on these long trips you would end up with a mouth full of bugs if you didn't wear a face guard of some form.

Morning rush hour traffic had died down as they navigated the outer suburbs of the Phoenix metro heading east. Luckily in Arizona motorcycles could use the carpool lanes to save time so that's what the pair chose to do. During their club days they had mastered the art of riding very fast, only feet away from each other, and Johnny was pleased to see they soon fell back into that old habit.

They cleared the outskirts of the Phoenix Metro and were soon on the open road. *Fuck.* Johnny realized how much he had missed this. The feeling of freedom and just traveling was the reason he had gotten into bikes in the first place, Sure, cars were "safer" and more comfortable, but nothing beat becoming one with your machine as you raced down the highway at seventy-five miles per hour. *We should do this more often,* he thought to himself as he avoided a Mack Truck in the slow lane.

About an hour into their ride, Joe signaled to Johnny that he wanted to stop. The rest stop was ahead so they made a bee line for the exit and pulled off. They found a spot to park where their bikes should not get run over by some tourist and pulled off their helmets.

"Fuck! I had forgotten how much I missed this," exclaimed Joe.

"Yeah, tell me about it, one thing is for sure we have to do more road trips after this one," Jonny replied.

The pair walked stiffly to the men's room.

"Damn man. I am pretty much seized up right now," declared Joe.

"I hear that," Johnny responded, stomping his legs to try and get the blood flow moving again.

After they hit the rest room the duo checked out the vending machines to see what was on offer. Even though summer was "officially" over it was still in the high '90s and Johnny bought them both sodas to hydrate.

"Thanks brother," said Joe when Johnny handed him his can. "Let's just sit here and drink these before we move on."

"Sounds good to me," said Johnny. "We have plenty of time."

They sat on a bench and watched all the travelers coming and going from their cars to the restrooms and back on the freeway again. Joe made disparaging comments about half of them, which had Johnny in stitches laughing.

They finished their sodas and Joe announced he had to go piss again. Johnny shrugged and thought, *Might as well go too.* Who knows when they would be stopping next.

CHAPTER TEN

As they rode down the I-10 freeway heading east Joe reflected on Johnny's state of mind. He hadn't seen his club brother this happy in years. This is where Johnny belonged–on his scoot and on the road.

They had pretty much both joined the Steel Reapers MC in their early twenties. The club was a lot more serious in the early '80s. If they were not fighting with other clubs, they would fight amongst themselves. He once witnessed Johnny knock out two guys from the Flagstaff chapter of their club for joking about the Steel Reapers. Club life was a serious business back then, and you defended the patch at all costs.

Things had changed by the mid-2000s. Was it a "kinder, gentler" world? Joe didn't know, but club members would do anything to avoid getting into beefs with other clubs or even the general public. Joe recalled a time on a road trip when they had stopped for a few beers somewhere in California. A couple of guys had made disparaging remarks against the club and none of the young club guys would say shit. It took Johnny and Joe to beat them senseless as the younger guys looked on.

Shortly after that, Johnny met with the club president and told him he was leaving the club. Of course, Joe followed suit. No Johnny, no club as far as Joe was concerned. Johnny was out good at first meaning he could still associate with current members. But inexplicably a few months later, the president hit up Johnny and told him he was out bad. No further contact was allowed between him and anyone in the club. Johnny would never admit it, but that decision crushed him. It took something away from him, and he wasn't the same after that.

Joe thought about it some more as they barreled down the highway. He understood fully that things were different back in the 1980s. You could get away with blue murder back then and rarely get caught. These days, soon as trouble started onlookers would whip out their cell phones and start recording you. If it wasn't cellphones, it was the god damn security cameras. They seemed to have them everywhere these days. Unless of course *your* bike got stolen, then for some reason, no cameras saw anything. Funny how that worked out.

Despite the camera excuse, Joe wondered if kids today were cut with a different cloth then those born in the 1960s. He recalled a friend of his, an ex-military man, telling him a story once. He was a lifelong soldier, now retired and his oldest son had signed up to follow in the old man's footsteps. After basic training he was allowed to go visit his son. His son was proudly showing his dad his bed and footlocker in the barracks. As he opened his footlocker, Joe's friend spotted a card that looked like something from a monopoly game lying on top of his son's personal possessions. When Dad asked his son what the card was all about, his son explained to him that if the drill Sargent was shouting at them too much, they could produce that card and be excused from verbal abuse for the day!

Both Joe's buddy and Joe were incredulous. Wasn't that the point of the Drill Sargent? To toughen you up. Excusing yourself from his shouting defeated the purpose. Joe shook his head. Maybe Johnny was right, kids these days were too soft.

As Joe was reflecting, he saw Johnny waving at him, giving him the agreed upon signal to stop at the next exit. What had it been? A little over an hour? Maybe Johnny was stopping to get something to eat. The signs for food and restaurants were pointing a mile or so down the road. Joe hated that. He preferred the truck stops where you pull off the freeway and get straight back on. No need to drive a few miles out of the way and back to the freeway again. Oh well, maybe Johnny needed to piss?

They pulled up in front of a McDonald's. Okay, maybe Johnny did want food.

Johnny pulled off his helmet and turned to Joe.

"Fuck, gotta piss again, damn soda went straight through me. We might as well grab some food while we are here, eh?"

"Sounds good to me," Joe replied. He tapped his knuckles against his gas tank. "Probably could do with gassing up after as well." He noted there was a gas station across the street from where they were parked.

"Yeah, cool," said Johnny, scurrying inside to try and find that bathroom.

CHAPTER ELEVEN

After eating lunch and gassing up, the duo rejoined the road that led back to the freeway. Johnny loved this part of the world. He felt like every mountain range had probably been featured in a Western movie that he watched as a kid. Well, if they hadn't been used then they should have been used, so picturesque. Shit, why didn't they make Westerns anymore? He felt like every Saturday afternoon as a child watching TV there would be a classic Western from the '40s, '50s and '60s shown on his little black and white TV. These days it was all 200-million-dollar superhero films that bored him senseless. It wasn't like he didn't like characters like Spiderman and Iron man, he had grown up reading those comic books like most kids, but it was the overuse of CGI effects that ruined the movies for him. What happened to a good storyline and a few effects versus the one hundred million things all going off on the big screen at the same time. Instead of wooing him it bored him senseless.

Despite their frequent bathroom breaks they were making good time and soon passed his old stomping ground of Tucson. Part of him felt a love hate relationship with Tucson. He had spent his formative years there and would have probably never left until his bitch of an ex-wife, Amanda, announced one day she "wasn't happy anymore" and packed up and took the kids to Phoenix. He had followed to stay in his kid's lives and over the years grew to love Phoenix. There was certainly more to see and do there compared to Tucson but now that he was getting older, something about the slower pace of life did appeal to him. There were still walking communities in Tucson where you didn't need a bike or car to get around and of course the cost of living was significantly cheaper too. Despite the small size of the city versus Phoenix, Tucson had some of the best food in the entire USA in Johnny's mind.

As they raced along further down the I-10 heading east, Johnny saw the signs for Tombstone. Due to all the precious metals that were mined there in the 1800s Tombstone had the honor of being the second largest city on the West Coast of America after San Francisco. These days it was kind of a ghost town with tourism pretty much being the only thing bringing in money for the townsfolk. He had done a school tour as a kid and been back as an adult. Johnny always figured if bikers were around in those days, they would have taken over Tombstone,

They stopped again to hit the rest room, take a break and re-hydrate. Heatstroke in Arizona was no joke, and even if you were not sweating it paid to get some liquids into you at every stop to ensure you didn't get messed up. Johnny had it once or twice before, just mild cases, and it had him bedridden for days. He noticed getting off his bike at the quick stop that he was much more stiff and sore than he used to be on long road trips. His back wasn't hurting yet, but he assumed it was coming. By his calculations they would be in Las Cruces in the next two hours. Could they make it before he needed another bathroom break? Only his bladder knew.

The duo made it the last two hours without having to stop and take a piss. Johnny honestly felt since they crossed the state line into New Mexico the scenery was nowhere near as impressive as the ride from Phoenix to Tucson, but whatever, they were not there for a sightseeing tour. Soon they started seeing chain restaurants and other signs of civilization. They had made it to town. First leg of the journey was pretty much done, just had to find their motel. Riding through town bought back all sorts of memories of growing up in Tucson. Las Cruces kind of felt like Tucson did in the '70s. Pretty cool, he thought.

Finally, they found their motel and parked up to check in. Johnny's legs and back were feeling it now. *How the hell did we do cross country trips on hard tail choppers back in the day?* he thought. I guess we were thirty years younger.

Check in at the motel was fairly pain free and they rode their scoots through the car park to find their room. Once they found it, they pulled off their bikes and checked out the room. Two beds, a TV set and a bathroom. Fairly standard motel room set up. Not bad for the price they were paying.

They dumped their bags in the room and made plans to go for a walk, go find food and most importantly, get their legs working to pump some blood back into them. As they were leaving Johnny surveyed the car park.

"Hey, maybe we should think of bringing the bikes inside?" he asked.

Joe looked around; a couple of sketchy characters were hanging out on the upstairs balconies.

"Sure, let's do it," he replied.

Took them a couple of minutes but they soon had both bikes parked inside. It was going to suck watching TV that night or even making it to the bathroom, navigating around two bikes in the dark, but hey, better than having some crackhead steal their rides in the middle of the night.

Satisfied their bikes would be safe they walked the neighborhood seeking out a good taco joint.

"Lots of churches in this town," commented Joe.

"You do know what Las Cruces means, don't you?" asked Johnny.

"Nah, what?" asked Joe.

"The Crosses," Johnny laughed.

"Oh, I see, well, that would explain it eh?" Joe laughed too.

CHAPTER TWELVE

It felt good to walk and get their legs moving. Johnny had no real clue where they were heading. It had been a long time since he had last stayed in Las Cruces. He just figured they would head down the street until the found some good Mexican food and stop and eat.

"What's up with all this Billy the Kid stuff everywhere?" asked Joe. "Was he born here?"

Johnny thought for a moment. "Nah, I don't think he was. I wanna say maybe New York City?"

"Was he killed here then?" asked Joe.

"I don't think he was killed here, but definitely somewhere in New Mexico. I guess he just spent a lot of time here. Let's face it, the Southwest was a lot wilder than NYC in those days," Johnny explained.

Joe pondered on everything Johnny had said. "Yeah, that makes sense. Hey, let's try this place the tacos look good," he said, pointing at a small family run restaurant to their left.

The two bikers went in and checked out the menu–both decided to order some Birria Tacos and some drinks. Joe ordered a Jarritos and Johnny ordered a Mexican coke. He always preferred the natural sugar of Mexican cokes.

After they devoured their dinner, Joe noticed there was a bar across the street.

"Hey Ace, you wanna have a beer?" he said, pointing out the dive bar across the street-smart.

Johnny looked over and thought for a moment. "Sure, but just one. Nothing too crazy, we gotta clear the border tomorrow, remember."

"Yeah. How could I forget. Yeah, one beer works for me. Just to chill out ya know?" Joe replied.

"Alright, let me finish my beverage and we will head over," Johnny said.

Johnny finished his Mexican coke, and they exited the family restaurant to grab some beers.

Johnny scanned the room entering the bar, old habit from his outlaw biker days. Threat assessment or whatever you call it. Couple of young guys drinking at the bar and a few old timers in one of the booths, but nothing to concern themselves with.

Johnny went to grab a booth in the corner of the room and positioned himself with his back against the wall so he could watch everyone coming and going. Old habits die hard and all that. Joe hit the bar and ordered a couple of PBRs plus two Whiskey shots. What the hell, they would finish these and go straight back to their room. No harm, no foul.

Joe returned and handed Johnny his beer and shot of whiskey.

"You fucker." Johnny laughed, looking at his whiskey shot.

"No biggie." Joe shrugged. "We can drink these and get an early night."

"You know it." Johnny smiled, chinking his glass to Joe's and pounding his whiskey.

"Ahh delicious." He laughed, taking a sip of beer to wash the taste down.

"Cheers," Joe replied, doing his shot too.

The old friends sat and enjoyed their beers, telling tales about the old days.

When their beers were over Johnny looked at the empty glasses and announced, "Fuck it, one more and then we go back to the motel."

"Well, alright," was all Joe could say as Johnny grabbed their empties and headed up to the bar.

Johnny soon returned with two more beers *and* two shots. Joe didn't say anything, and he certainly wasn't going to turn down free liquor from Johnny. Johnny was always known as being a tight wad when it came to his turn to buy drinks and Joe wasn't going to miss the opportunity to take advantage of his current situation. He toasted Johnny and necked his shot of whiskey. Tasted even better than the last one. They picked up their conversation about the old days and whatever happened to old friends from the '80s.

Out of the blue Johnny turned to Joe with a very serious look on his face.

"You got my back bro?" he asked Joe.

"Always, bro. You know that. What's up?" he questioned.

"There is a young guy at the bar who keeps looking over at us. He's a one percenter but I can't make out his club colors," explained Ace.

"What's he doing?" asked Joe, tempted to look back over his shoulder.

"He's with two guys and he keeps looking over at us and making eye contact," explained Johnny. "If he keeps staring this way, he's gonna get a beat down."

"Well, let's just see what he does," suggested Joe, trying to be the voice of reason.

That seemed to cool Johnny down, at least for the next five minutes. The last thing Joe wanted right now was a massive bar fight, especially after the first day of their road trip.

"Right, that does it!" exclaimed Johnny. "He's looking over again. I'm gonna finish this beer, pretend to return it to the bar and smash it over his head!"

Joe swore under his breath. "Oh great, here we go again."

He risked looking back over his shoulder to check this guy out. There he was by the bar, maybe twenty-four, twenty-five definitely under thirty. Leather vest on, Joe could see his diamond one percenter patch on his right shoulder from the booth they were sitting in.

"Let me handle this brother," said Joe, grabbing their empties and heading back to the bar.

He squeezed between the young biker and his two friends.

'Two more please," he asked the barmaid. Then, turning to the guy who had been looking over at them, he asked, "What's up?"

"Hey, nice to meet ya. You guys are Steel Reapers, right?" the young guy asked.

Joe eyed the guy up and down, certainly didn't give off cop vibes. "Who's asking?"

"Oh shit, sorry, I'm Kurt. I ride for the Forsaken Brotherhood MC." Kurt extended his hand.

Joe took it and shook, firm grip.

"Forsaken Brotherhood? Oh, you guys are a New Mexico support club for the Reapers, right?" asked Joe.

"Yeah, that's right!" Kurt smiled. "I think I met you guys when I was a prospect."

"Well, you've for a good memory, that must have been four to five years ago, yeah?"

"I've been fully patched in for four years now, so yeah." Kurt smiled.

"Congrats." Joe smiled too. "Nice to meet ya." Joe grabbed his beers from the bar maid and paid for his drinks.

"Can I get you anything?" asked Kurt.

"Well, I just got these." Joe shrugged, thinking, *Well, he could have offered to pay for these before I did, cheap fucker.*

"Ah yeah, sorry," commented Kurt.

Joe returned to their booth and Johnny.

"He's cool bro, local club guy. New Mexico support club for the Reapers," explained Joe.

"Ah okay then," said Johnny, still not sounding 100 percent convinced.

"Says he met us when he was a prospect and we were running with the Reapers," Joe continued.

Johnny still wasn't convinced but kept his mouth shut and sipped on his new beer.

They were halfway done with their beers when Joe heard someone approaching. He turned just in time to see their new friend Kurt approaching with some whiskey shots. Without asking he slid into the booth next to Joe.

49

"Hey fellas, just want to show my respect by bringing you some shots," Kurt explained.

"Kurt, this is Johnny, most people call him Ace though. Johnny, this is the guy I was telling you about. Kurt from the Forsaken Brotherhood club," Joe introduced him.

"Hey Kurt," said Johnny, taking a whiskey shot from the young biker.

The three bikers "cheersed" each other and downed their shots.

"Fuck, I need a chaser," announced Kurt, getting up top head back to the bar.

Johnny looked at Joe, almost to challenge him, and Joe shrugged back, almost a "Let's just see where this goes" kind of attitude.

Kurt quickly returned with a new beer for himself and two more for Joe and Johnny.

"Here you go guys," he said, sliding fresh beers over to the older bikers.

"Thanks," was all Johnny said, still nursing his earlier beer.

"So, what brings you boys to Las Cruces?" asked Kurt.

Even though Joe didn't get cop vibes from the guys, he wasn't dumb, and he wasn't going to volunteer any more info that he had to.

"Ah, we are just roading tripping to catch up on some old friends," Joe explained. "Just passing through town on the way there."

"Very cool." Kurt smiled. "You can't beat a good road trip."

"That's for sure," Joe replied.

The trio swapped road stories and finished their beers. Without asking, Johnny got up and came back with three more beers. Halfway through the next beer Joe announced, "Ah that's gonna be it for me tonight, I'm getting pretty buzzed."

"Ahh I got you covered man," said Kurt. Before Joe or Johnny had a chance to reply, Kurt pulled out a baggy of cocaine and his buck knife. He dipped the knife into the bag and held the white powder under Joe's nose. The look of surprise on Johnny's face was priceless.

"What? Here? Now?" asked Joe, incredulous.

"Yeah, it's fine. No one here will rat us out, believe me," reassured Kurt.

Joe snorted half the powder up one nostril and the remainder using his other nostril.

"Whooo," he shouted. Kurt laughed.

Kurt dipped his knife in again and handed it over to Johnny. "Here you go."

Johnny took his bumps and handed the knife back.

"Whoa, that's some good shit, thank you brother," Johnny said.

"Fresh over the border guys, super clean not cut with anything." Kurt smiled.

"Yeah, I can tell," said Joe with a big goofy grin on his face. "Thanks again."

Kurt did a couple of bumps and returned his baggie. He wiped his knife down on his jeans and returned his blade.

Revitalized, the trio kept drinking and shooting the shit. Joe even went up and ordered another round of beers and shots for the table.

After that round of shots and beers, Kurt did the same trick of pulling out his knife and baggy to give the guys another "pick me up," if you will.

Their stories of bar fights and girls they had known along the way got more and more wild as the jenkem and alcohol flowed. Even Johnny was enjoying himself. Before they knew it, it was the last call.

Kurt got one final round in for everyone, and they all traded cell numbers.

"You boys know how to find your way back to your hotel?" asked Kurt.

"Yeah, I am pretty sure we do," said Johnny. "We're like a five-minute walk away."

"Hey, thanks for the hospitality," complimented Joe. "Hit us up next time you are in Phoenix and we will return the favor."

"Thanks guys, much appreciated." Kurt smiled.

They exited the bar and Kurt staggered to his Harley.

"Hey, you good to ride bro?" asked Joe.

"Yeah, I only live a few miles away, I'll be fine," Kurt replied. With that he straddled his bike and fired it up. Joe watched him pull out of the car park, a little wobbly at first but soon rectified the situation and tore off up the street.

Johnny looked around trying to remember which way they had come from.

"Okay. We gotta cross back over the street and we are down that way," he said, pointing the way they had come hours ago.

Somehow, they made their way home. It always surprised Joe what a great "beer compass" Johnny had that he could be three sheets to the wind in a strange town and always manage to find his way back to where they were staying. His beer compass had never failed them before.

Joe took a piss, washed his face and got into his bed. Johnny realized then that he had chosen the bed furthest from the bathroom. He sighed, realizing it was going to be a long night. He should have stuck with the one beer they swore they were going to drink.

They had managed to position their bikes running parallel to their individual beds so at least he had a clear path to the bathroom as he was sure he would be back and forth all night emptying his aging bladder.

Johnny washed his face and staggered into his bed. He wondered if he would be able to get any sleep with the effects of all the cocaine still coursing through his body. Finally, the booze beat out the coke and he passed out. He woke up an hour later, at first confused as to where he was. He could hear Joe snoring in the other bed and realized he was in the motel. He tried to get up and go piss again, stubbing his left foot's small toe on the rear wheel of Joe's scoot en route to the bathroom. He had to suppress his cursing to avoid waking up Joe.

Shit, fuck shit, he swore quietly to himself inside the bathroom. He took a piss and walked like a blind man without a cane back into his bed.

It seemed like no sooner had he put his head down again when there was a loud pounding at their door.

"Hey, hey, time to check out guys, let's go," shouted a voice from outside the door.

Johnny was furious. He felt like shit and needed to rest.

"Check out is at 11 a.m. asshole, come back then!" he shouted.

"It's 11:45 a.m., you gotta go," the voice replied.

"Like fuck it is," Johnny shouted back. He reached for his phone on the nightstand and checked the time. *Shit, it was 11:45 a.m.*

Johnny groaned. "Joe. Offer him another twenty dollars so we can get a late check out. I need more sleep."

Joe jumped out of bed only wearing his boxers and grabbed his wallet. He stepped outside letting in a blinding blast of daylight.

"Ugh shut the damn door already," signed Johnny.

He could hear Joe outside talking to the motel manager.

He quickly returned. "Okay, we got two more hours."

Just like that, Joe was in bed and snoring again. Johnny felt a pang of jealousy. Knowing his luck, he would fall back asleep at 1:55 p.m.

The next thing he knew Joe was shaking him awake.

"Hey c'mon man it's 2:30 p.m., we gotta go," Joe explained.

"Ugh I feel like dog shit," groaned Johnny. "Why do we do this to ourselves?'

"You tell me brother. Story of our lives." Joe laughed, who apparently had already showered and shaved.

CHAPTER THIRTEEN

Johnny took a quick shower and still felt like shit. He threw his clothes on, and they managed to wheel their bikes out of the motel room without any issues. They were finally ready to leave.

"Should we try and find somewhere with an all-day breakfast?" asked Joe. "A Denny's or something?"

"Nah. I'm way too shaky to eat right now bro," Johnny replied. "I could do with a fountain soda, that always seems to help. What say we find a gas station, top up our tanks and get some hydration?"

Joe thought for a moment. "Okay then, I'm kinda hungry though."

How the fuck could anyone be hungry right now? thought Johnny.

Johnny saw the pained look on Joe's face.

"Look man, we should be at the old man's place in ninety minutes. I'm sure he will take us to a kick ass Mexican food place. We can eat then, alright?" Johnny explained.

"Aww, I guess I can wait." Joe shrugged. "I recall a gas station back down the road if ya wanna circle back, okay?"

"Okay cool, I'll follow you then," Johnny said, sliding on his helmet.

Sure enough, after two blocks they found a QT gas station, topped up their tanks, parked and went to get sodas. For some reason a can or plastic bottle of coke didn't have the same effect on Johnny as a fountain soda. They were the only ones that seemed to help his hangover. No clue why, that's just the way it was.

They sat on the curb in front of the gas station finishing their beverages. Johnny noticed Joe had bought a protein bar and a banana to deal with his hunger pains. Fair enough.

"I guess I'll text the Old Man and let him know we're running late," suggested Johnny.

He opened his Telegram app and texted, explaining they were running late.

In seconds, Hank replied with a simple, "Okay. See you in a few."

"Okay we are all good," said Johnny. "With any luck we'll be there in a little over an hour."

"Alright, can't wait," Joe replied. "I'm starving. I'm sure Hank will take us for some killer food."

Johnny looked at his GPS app on his phone.

"Okay, so it looks pretty easy," he explained. "A straight shot down the I-10 past El Paso and we are there."

"Nice," said Joe. "Ya got ya passport, right?"

Johnny patted his cargo pants pocket. "Yep."

"Shall we get going then?" asked Joe.

"Sure," Johnny replied. Standing up he realized he had to hit the bathroom again. "Fuck I gotta piss, gimmie a minute, would ya?"

Johnny headed back in to find the men's room as Joe waited outside by the bikes.

Pretty soon the duo was on their way headed south on the I-10 freeway. Traffic wasn't too bad; in fact, it felt like more people were heading north than south this afternoon, which pleased Johnny to no end as he was in no mood to deal with trucks or traffic jams right now.

CHAPTER FOURTEEN

Despite making good time, Johnny felt like shit. All he wanted to do was lie down and go back to sleep. All self-inflicted, of course. He should have never agreed to go to the bar with Joe. Whenever you set yourself a limit like "Just one beer and that's it," you pretty much cursed yourself to a night on the town. He should have eaten, gone back to the motel, watched some TV, and had an early night. Stupid, stupid, stupid. Then again, he had pretty much lived his life instinctively for as long as he could remember. Look where that had gotten him. A failed marriage, kids who hated him, a mid-level job and financial problems. But a lot of his friends and peers growing up were dead or in prison. So in that respect, maybe he wasn't doing so bad after all?

They rode on. Soon they were seeing signs for El Paso. They would be in Mexico before they knew it.

Joe pointed at the sign and gave the thumbs up, clearly excited for the next leg in their travels.

Without even checking his GPS the pair managed to find the TX-375 Loop to Juarez. *They certainly made it easy for people to find their way,* thought Johnny as they rode on. In his mind he was planning to get to old man

Hank's place, get some great tasting food, take a shower and get an early night.

He thought back to the days where they would stay up for two to three days at a time partying and still make it back to work on time Monday morning. *Ah, to be young and dumb again.* Johnny smiled at the idea.

They peeled off the loop and found themselves in line to the point of entry into Mexico with a few cars in front of them. They rolled ahead slowly, and soon they were crossing to the Mexican side of the Rio Grande and were met with two officials who waved them over to the side.

WTF, thought Johnny. *Is this normal?*

They were charged forty dollars each for an entry fee which they both paid. Luckily the old man had warned them of this.

The uniformed workers asked Joe and Johnny if they were bringing in more than 10,000 dollars cash and if they were carrying firearms, both of which the pair told the guards that they did not.

"You have tip?" asked the one official in broken English.

"You want a tip?" asked Johnny incredulously. "Sheesh." *Some people want money for nothing these days!*

He shook his head at the guy.

"Tip, tip," he insisted.

Johnny was starting to get pissed off. *I ain't paying a guy a tip for taking my entrance fee, screw him.*

"No tip, no tip," he replied.

The official looked shocked, and his partner was starting to get agitated.

Just as Johnny figured they were going to end up in a Mexican prison another biker pulled up behind them. Clearly this man had done the border crossing before and could see what the problem was.

"Problems fellas?" the new arrival asked Joe and Johnny.

"Yeah, this fucker wants a tip from us!" explained Joe.

"No, no. He means your T.I.P." The biker laughed.

"Our what?" asked Johnny.

"Oh, your Temporary Import Permit," explained the biker. You gotta show the Mexican authorities you aren't bringing your bike in to sell it but will be riding it out when you leave."

"Ahh like a Carnet in Europe?" suggested Joe.

"Yes, exactly," confirmed the biker.

When did Joe ever travel to Europe? thought Johnny. *That sneaky fucker.*

"So where do we get these TIPS?" asked Joe.

"On the USA side I think," explained the biker, pulling out his paperwork to show the Mexican officials. "I applied for mine online via the Mexican Consulate."

"Ah cool, thanks for the help," Johnny said.

"Yeah, no problem." The biker smiled. "Hey! Be warned, it cost me 400 dollars and you gotta have your registration and your title."

Johnny thought for a second. Did he bring his title? He was sure he had it with his registration.

"400? Get out of here!" Johnny cursed.

"No, no. It's fully refundable. When you come back and they see you never sold your bike," explained the biker.

The immigration officials had finished processing the biker's paperwork and were telling him was now free to leave.

"Hey, I gotta go, good luck fellas and a word of advice…"

"What's that?" asked Joe.

"Switch your speedo from miles to kilometers before you get going. Too easy to get a ticket here if you ride in miles."

"Hey, good idea, thanks brother. Safe travels," Joe replied.

The pair spent the rest of the afternoon running back and forth between the USA side and the Mexican side of the border until they finally got all their paperwork in order and were cleared for travel.

Despite the friendly biker explaining to them that the TIP fee was fully refundable on their return to the USA, Johnny had mentally kissed that money goodbye. He knew damn well they would not be legally crossing back over the border on their return to the United States.

After hours of messing about they were finally rolling into Juarez. The first thing Johnny noticed was the amount of potholes compared to the El Paso side. Other than that, it actually looked pretty similar to most of the border towns on the US side that Johnny had visited.

Joe was waving for him to pull over. *What now?* thought Johnny. The duo pulled up in front of a row of stores.

"We should hit the ATM and get some Pesos, Ace," suggested Joe.

"Actually, that's a good idea," Johnny replied. They parked their bikes and found a touristy looking place to withdraw some local currency.

After getting some cash, they grabbed a couple of ice-cold beverages to rehydrate with. Standing next to their bikes, Joe commented, "I could have done without all that administration BS but at least we're here now, eh?"

"That we are my old friend." Johnny smiled. "I'll text Hank to let him know we're here now and punch his home address into my GPS, okay?"

"Sounds good," said Joe, finishing his soda and dumping the empty cup into a trash can.

CHAPTER FIFTEEN

After finishing their beverages, it took them about fifteen minutes to find the old man's place. Johnny was surprised it looked just like a nice suburban house that you might find in Tucson. *Well okay then,* he thought to himself.

As they were pulling in the old man himself came out and waved at them. Johnny figured he must have heard the motorcycles and known it was them. He stepped down off the front porch and undid the side gate so they could pull their bikes up the side of the house's driveway and park them out back. He closed the gate behind them and gestured towards the back of the house.

The two followed and parked at the back of his premises. Hank had followed behind them after locking the gate. He was all smiles.

"Wow! Good to see ya both, it's been a few years."

"I reckon twenty years," suggested Joe.

"Wow, really? That long? That's crazy. You both look good," he said.

"Thanks brother, great to see you too," Johnny replied, noticing the old man's thinning hair and larger beer belly.

"Our scoots gonna be safe back here?" asked Joe.

"Yeah of course, you'll be fine," Hank replied. "It's a good neighborhood."

"Okay cool," said Joe, shutting off his bike and dismounting.

"I thought Juarez was dangerous?" asked Johnny.

"Well, yeah, to be honest when I first moved here twenty years ago it was pretty dangerous in parts, but in general, that's all calmed down now, ya know?" Hank explained.

"Okay good to know," Johnny replied.

"I was expecting you guys earlier," stated Hank. "Everything go okay?"

Joe laughed. "Well, we had a bit of a slow start today."

"Haha, I figured as much." Hank laughed.

"Plus, we got fucked at the border," said Johnny. "TIPs forms and all that."

"Oh yeah, I forgot about those. My bike was bought in Mexico so I don't have to deal with that," explained Hank.

"Ahh, that makes sense. I was wondering why ya didn't warn us," Johnny responded.

"Well, you could have checked any 'Travel to Mexico' website, Ace." Hank laughed. "Anyways, let me show ya to your rooms."

"Rooms? We have separate rooms?" Joe enquired. "Wow, luxury."

"Grab your gear and let me give you the guided tour," said Hank. "I imagine you guys are hungry. You want to dump your gear, shower and then I can take you for food?"

"Food? Now you're talking," said Joe. "I'm always down for good food."

"Well in that case, I got ya covered," said Hank, holding the back door open so the pair could enter his house.

Johnny and Joe dumped their gear in their respective rooms, took turns having showers and changed their clothes. After they were ready, they walked down the street with Hank leading the way to a local family run Mexican taco place.

A man who Johnny assumed to be the owner led them to a table.

"Hola señor Carter, siempre es un placer verlo. ¿Tú y tus amigos necesitan ver menús?" he asked.

What in tarnation? thought Johnny. He heard, "Hello Mister Carter" and that was about all he could figure out.

Joe and Johnny looked at the old man with perplexed expresión on their faces.

"Oh shit." Hank laughed. "You two fuckers don't speak Spanish, do you?"

Johnny shrugged. "I understand about two words. I thought everyone speaks English these days."

Hank turned to the owner. "Sí señor, definitivamente necesitaremos menús."

"Let me guess, you asked him for menus?" questioned Joe.

"Very good." Hank chuckled. "Shit, I just thought of something. You guys can't speak Spanish so I'm assuming you can't read it either. Just tell me what you want, and I will order on your behalf."

"Yeah, that's gonna help," Johnny replied.

"I guess a bunch of tacos and a beer for me," said Johnny.

"That works for me too," Joe added.

Old man Hank made the order and a young waitress, possibly the owner's daughter, brought them out some chips and salsa to start with. Moments later, she returned with three margaritas.

"What's this?" asked Johnny.

"Tequila boys. Come on, you can't be in Mexico and not at least have a Margarita. I'll order beers next round."

Johnny grabbed a chip and dunked it into the salsa and took a bite.

"Wow, that's gotta be the best chips and salsa I've ever had."

"Not bad, eh?" smiled Hank.

He picked up his margarita glass and cheersed the two younger bikers.

"So just you and your wife live down here?" asked Johnny after half his 'rita.

"Nah, just me. Rosita passed two years ago," said Hank

"Oh damn. Sorry for your loss bro," said Joe. "Covid?"

"No, cancer," said Hank.

"Shit, sorry man," said Johnny. "Why not move back home?"

"You know, I've been here twenty years now. No way I could afford to return and live in the US anymore. My social security check goes so much further here than it ever would in the USA," Hank explained

"Yeah, I guess you got a point," said Joe.

The waitress brought over their food, and they started eating. Johnny thought these were the best tasting Tacos he had ever had. No wonder the old man had stayed down here; the food was off the charts.

After dinner the waitress took their plates and brought them fresh margaritas.

"So what's our plan for the week then?" asked Johnny.

The old man took a swig of his drink.

"We gotta head south. Sinaloa actually," Hank explained. "It's a two-day ride to Durango, then we pick up. Head down to Mazatlan, maybe stay there for a day or so. Then another two days' ride north to get you boys back to Nogales and I'll head east at that point to head home."

Johnny did a quick calculation in his head. "So, we're talking about five days then?"

Hank thought for a moment. "Yeah, give or take. That sounds right."

"Gonna be epic," said Joe. "Let's get some tequila shots."

Hank ordered the tequila shots, and the boys washed them down with more beers. After that Hank called the owner over, said something to him in fluent Spanish, and paid the bill.

"This one is on me boys–shall we head back to the house?" he said.

"Hey man, thanks for dinner. That was awesome," said Joe.

"Yeah man, thanks brother," added Johnny. "I'll get you dinner tomorrow."

"Thanks fellas. It's been great to see ya both after all this time," Hank replied. "Let's get back to the house."

The trio made the short walk back to the house and Hank ushered them into the living room. He pulled out a pocket-sized road map from a bookshelf, left it on his coffee table and disappeared into the kitchen.

Hank returned with a couple more beers, passing two to Joe and Johnny.

"Here ya go fellas, check this out."

He pulled the map open, spread it out over the coffee table and pointed to it.

"We are here, Juarez. Tomorrow we will ride to Chihuahua," he explained.

"Chihuahua? Like the dog? Is that where they came from?" asked Joe.

"Yeah, I think you're right," said Johnny. "From memory the Spanish explorers found them in that area. Smallest dogs in the world or something."

"Yeah, you're both right," said Hank. "Apparently, they have ancient rare dog DNA that doesn't exist in any other breed."

"No shit," said Joe. "I always hated those little fuckers, either super nervous or super crazy."

Hank and Johnny laughed.

"So, we will be staying in Chihuahua over night?" asked Johnny.

"Yeah. It's about a six hour ride. If we factor in food, gas, bathroom breaks and tolls it'll probably take us seven to eight hours," Hank explained.

"I got ya," said Johnny, thinking back to their run from Phoenix to Las Cruces.

"What's Chihuahua like?" asked Joe.

"It's a pretty cool city," said Hank. "If you factor in the metro area it's probably around two million people I would say. Got some cool colonial architecture too."

"That would be good to see if we have time," Joe replied.

"Is it gonna be hot down there?" asked Johnny.

Hank thought for a moment. "Hmm, usually this time of year around eighty-five degrees I would say. Light jacket and riding vest?"

"That's not bad," said Johnny. "I just brought my leather so I won't be sweltering."

Joe finished his beer. "Hey brother, any more beers in the fridge?"

Hank stood up. "Lemme go look."

Johnny turned to Joe. "Looks like it will be a good first day ride in Mexico, brother."

"Yeah, I'm looking forward to exploring it. I've only ever been to Nogales and TJ," Joe replied.

Hank returned with three whiskey tumblers.

"What's this?" asked Johnny.

"Tequlia bro," Hank explained. "I'm all out of beers."

"You can't expect me to do that as a shot," Johnny said incredulously.

"No, no," Hank replied. "You boys are in Mexico now. This is how Tequila is meant to be drunk, like

Americans drink a whiskey. Only American college kids drink it as shots."

Johnny wasn't sure if that was right or not. "Okay, if you say so," he said, sipping on his drink.

"So, you are all good to do this run with us?" asked Joe.

"Of course, man, what else am I gonna do?" Hank smiled. "I can't keep just sitting here waiting to die, ya know?"

"Ha, I guess," said Joe. "Well, who knows, if this goes well maybe we will do it a few more times, eh?"

"That would be cool," said Hank.

"So, what made you come down here anyways?" asked Johnny. "I thought your girl was American?"

"She was Mexican American," Hank explained. "Her dad was doing poorly so she wanted to spend some time with him before he passed. Besides..."

"Besides what?" asked Johnny.

"Well, you remember the big bust for the Steel Reapers, right?" said Hank.

"Dave and Tommy?" asked Joe.

"Yeah, I was partners with them," Hank explained. "My nerves couldn't take it—every night I would have dreams we were going to get busted."

'Oh shit," said Joe.

"Yeah, don't get me wrong, the money was great, but I was a wreck, looking over my shoulder at every turn. Always convinced there was a rat amongst us," Hank continued.

"Turns out the rat was one of their buyers," said Johnny.

"Yeah, I heard. So anyways, when Rosita wanted to move down here to spend time with her father, I did one more deal with the boys. Cashed out, bought this place and then I heard the news. Terrible."

"Yeah man, the boys got thirty years each," said Joe. "Sounds like you got out just in time."

"I reckon I did," said Hank, raising his glass to his old friends.

"So after Chihuahua where do we go?" asked Johnny, wanting to get back to their travel plans before he got too wasted.

"Durango, Durango will be next," said Hank, still thinking about his friends serving hard time.

"What's that like?" asked Joe.

"Yeah, it's actually really nice. I think you guys will like it a lot." Hank smiled. "Anyone need a top up?"

Johnny looked at his glass. He was already drunk. How much more damage could one more do?

"Sure, why not?" he asked, handing his empty tumbler back to Hank.

Hank returned with three full glasses of tequila which he passed one each to both Joe and Johnny.

"Thanks man," said Joe, raising his glass. "Here's to road tripping with good brothers!"

Hank and Johnny raised their glasses too.

"So is it true about the water?" asked Joe.

"Eh, it depends province to province," Hank explained. "In general, tap water is okay for brushing your teeth, washing your hands, showering and stuff. But I would recommend drinking bottled water for hydration purposes, okay?"

"Wow, it's really that bad?" asked Johnny.

"Like I said, it varies town to town, so stick to beers or bottled water and you will be fine," said Hank. "I have a stack of bottled water in the fridge so feel free to grab some before you go to bed tonight."

The last time Johnny checked the clock before going to bed it was already well past 2 a.m. He had drunk way more than he had intended but at the end of the day he was catching up with an old club brother he hadn't seen in more than twenty years. It would have been poor form to sit there and not drink. He would deal with his life choices in the morning.

Heading to bed he was pleased to see that his bedroom had an en suite bathroom. *I am going to need that later,* he thought.

He hit the bed and probably passed out thirty seconds later. Sure enough, when he woke up it was still pitch black outside and he had to piss BAD. It took him a second to realize he was not at home but at old man Hank's place. He relieved himself and took a large drink of water from the bottle he had placed there earlier as his mouth was so dry. He realized he would probably have to get up again later to piss that out too, but oh well.

Johnny went back to bed and passed right out again. Sure enough, an hour later he was back up and staggering to the bathroom. *Fuck, just let me sleep already,* he cursed his aging body.

He kept the bathroom light off this time and could barely see the toilet bowl but could tell he was on target by the noise alone. Staggering back to bed he hoped that he would be able to fall asleep so easy again. He did. The next time he woke the sun was starting to peak over the horizon. *What would that be, 6 a.m.? Earlier?* He wasn't sure in this part of the world. He pissed yet again and dragged his weary ass back to bed. Hank said they were hoping to set off around 10 a.m. so he figured he would have a chance to get some much needed extra sleep.

When he finally woke up it was bright outside. The blinds in Hank's spare bedroom didn't do much to shield him from the sunlight. Outside of the room he could hear someone in the kitchen. *Fuck, I might as well get up,* he thought to himself. Truth is, he could have done with an entire day just lying in bed.

He took another piss and finished off the bottle of water he had left by the bathroom sink. Johnny pulled on a T-shirt and left the room to see who was up. He found both Hank and Joe sitting in Hank's kitchen.

"Here he is," Hank laughed.

"Get any rest?" asked Joe.

"Yeah some, could do with oh about eight hours more," Johnny replied.

"You hungry?" asked Hank. "I made you and Joe Huevos Rancheros."

"It's really good," commented Joe with a mouthful of food.

"Ugh no, just coffee for me," Johnny replied. "Thanks though."

"Your loss." Hank shrugged.

"Yeah, I can't face food right now," said Johnny. "I am sure I'll be starving in an hour or two though."

Hank spilt Johnny's portion of breakfast onto two plates, one for Joe and one for him. They sat and ate as Johnny sipped on his coffee.

"What time is it?" he asked.

"10:30 a.m.," Hank replied. "We should aim to leave around 11 a.m. so we get into Chihuahua before nightfall."

"Oh, it's that dangerous?" asked Joe.

"Nah, it's fine. My eyesight sucks and I hate riding at night these days," said Hank.

"Yeah, I feel that," said Johnny. "I could ride all night without issue back in the day, but these days I try and avoid night riding where possible. Especially in unfamiliar areas."

"Yeah, I get it," said Hank. "Trust me, I do."

"You old farts," said Joe.

"Hey, you're only two years younger than me, ya fucker." Johnny laughed.

Hank had finished eating now and grabbed his dirty dishes and took them to the sink. He cleaned his plates and put everything away.

"I'll grab my gear and be ready in ten minutes. So brush your teeth, take a piss, whatever you gotta do. Do it now."

"Will do Hank," said Joe.

Joe and Johnny retired to their respective rooms to re-pack their gear. In five minutes, both were ready. Hank soon joined them and led them out back. He locked his back door and went to the garage to retrieve his bike.

As he wheeled it, out Joe commented, "Well, I'll be! Hank 'The Old Man' Carter riding a Honda. I never thought I would see the day."

Johnny laughed.

"It's not a Honda you retards, it's an Italika," Hank shouted.

"Italika? What's that? An Italian bike?" asked Joe. "Never heard of them."

"Geez, you guys are ignorant," Hank replied, somewhat angrily. "It's only the most popular Motorcycle brand in Mexico."

"Oh shit, never heard of them," said Johnny. "Guess you been down here long enough, eh?"

"You know it." Hank smiled.

CHAPTER SIXTEEN

Hank went back into the garage to grab his gloves and helmet.

"You guys have Cardo packs, right?" he asked.

"Cardio packs?" asked Joe. "Hell no, why would we want to do cardio?"

"No dumbass, he means those wireless headsets to talk to each other on the road," Johnny corrected him.

"Oh," Joe replied. "No we don't, do you?"

"For fuck's sake," Hank replied. "How are we gonna talk to each other?"

"C'mon man, you're twenty years older than us. We do it like the good old days, with hand signals and gestures," said Johnny.

"Man, you guys are living like cavemen. Why don't you throw your phones away and just use pay phones?" Hank fumed.

"Cuz they don't have them anymore, dumbass," Joe replied.

"Hey, sometimes ya gotta embrace technology boys," said Hank, returning with another helmet.

"Look, if you need a bathroom break or gotta gas up just signal us," said Johnny. "It worked for us to get here."

"Oh boy, this is gonna be interesting. No Cardo packs and neither of you two geniuses speak Spanish." Hank shook his head.

Hank checked the pressure in his tires and gave his bike a quick once over to make sure no bolts had come loose since the last time he had ridden it. He tapped his gas tank.

"Hey, I gotta fill up before we hit the highway," he explained.

"No worries," said Johnny. "I could do with some more gas too, plus I need a fountain soda."

"Okay, there's a gas station two blocks away. We will hit that then the highway," said Hank. "Easy ride today. Just straight south on Highway 45."

"Cool," said Joe.

The trio pushed their bikes down the side of Hank's house and after opening the gate, they rolled them out to the street and fired them up. Johnny always liked to let his bike warm up for a moment before long rides.

They rolled out with Hank in the lead and sure enough, they were soon at the gas station filling their tanks. Johnny ran in and grabbed a large fountain soda to help with his hangover. He sat on the curb drinking it as the others stretched their legs. After finishing his soda, he gave a "wind up" time to go gesture. The trio fired up their bikes again and Hank gave the follow me gesture with his hand as they drove down the road towards the highway south.

They had managed about two blocks when Joe gave the sign that he had to pull over.

The restroom already? Though Johnny. *Geez, he's worse than me.*

They pulled over in the car park for an abandoned restaurant.

Johnny pulled off his helmet.

"What's up?" he asked.

"My bike died," exclaimed Joe.

Hank and Joe set up trouble shooting Joe's scoot. They checked the spark plugs, nothing. Hank pulled the fuel line and, nothing. Even blowing through — it nothing.

"Fuck!" swore Joe.

Hank looked worried.

Johnny went up to check the bike. He toggled the tank to the reserve switch. Gas started to flow again.

"You guys are dummies," he cursed. "Let's hit the road we are burning daylight."

"You ready?" Hank asked Joe as he got back on his bike.

"Yeah," he said, still red with embarrassment. "Let's go."

After another five minutes cruising through the suburbs of Juarez, Hank led them onto the ramp for the freeway south. They merged onto the highway and picked up speed. Johnny was surprised that Hank's little Mexican motorcycle was able to keep pace with his and Joe's far more powerful Harleys. *He must have modded it,* he thought to himself.

Johnny was enjoying riding in a foreign country; however, he couldn't help but marvel on how similar riding on the highways here was so similar to the freeways in Arizona. Except for the damn toll roads. It seemed like every couple of miles they would have to pay out some more pesos to keep riding. He wondered if that's why they were called freeways on the West Coast of the USA and highways on the East Coast (due to all the toll roads) cuz they certainly were not FREE.

About an hour had passed and he needed to piss again. He pulled in front of Hank and gave the signal. Hank nodded and they found a spot to pull off the highway.

It wasn't a truck stop but more of a rest area, no gas no food options.

Hank pulled off his helmet. "More bike problems?" he asked.

"Nah, gotta piss again," Johnny explained.

"Again? You only went about an hour ago son. Maybe you should get ya prostrate checked when you get home," Hank suggested.

"Nah, my prostate is just fine," Johnny snapped back. "It's just when I drink the night before. I sleep just fine on the nights I don't drink."

"Hmm, in that case maybe you're pre-diabetic then?" Hank replied.

"Yeah possibly, but I don't want to give up drinking," Johnny replied. "I'll just live with the consequences."

"Fair enough." Hank shrugged as he watched Johnny scuttle off to the bushes to relieve himself.

"What about you?" Hank asked Joe. "You gotta go too?"

"Nah, I'm good Hank," Joe replied.

Johnny rejoined them and just before they pulled out Hank told them, "There is a town called Villa Ahumada in about twenty minutes. We should stop there, gas up and maybe get lunch"

"Sounds good, I could do with breakfast actually," said Johnny. "I finally got my appetite."

"Yeah, let's do it," added Joe.

They made quick work of the next leg of the journey and followed Hank down the main street of the town. Soon he was signaling them to pull over.

'There's a good taco place here," he said after pulling off his helmet.

The trio parked up and entered the hole-in-the-wall taco spot. Joe and Johnny grabbed a table as Hank made an order for them all. He returned with some bottles of coke and sat down.

"How much was that, Hank?" offered Joe. "Here's some money."

"Thanks brother, always appreciated," said Hank, pocketing the pesos. "I've eaten here before. It's good."

A lady soon bought them their food and they all started eating. Between bites Hank asked the guys, "So you guys never told me, why did ya both leave the club?"

Johnny paused for a second, almost if he had to search for the right words.

"Look, don't get me wrong, I love the club, that was my family for almost thirty years," Johnny explained.

"I know, I was the same," Hank replied.

"But it just wasn't the same anymore," Johnny continued. "Remember Ronnie Two Toes and Blacktop Jimmy in the '80s?"

"Of course," Hank said.

"They both took thirty years for that bar fight that ended in that guy getting killed. Neither of them was responsible. In fact, the guy that did kill him took the stand and said he did it. The courts didn't believe him, and they got thirty years. Did they rat? Did they snitch? No, of course not," Johnny ranted.

"I remember that well. I went to court most of the days of the trial," Hank replied.

"That's backbone, Hank. Backbone. Younger guys get caught with a twenty dollar bindle of coke, and they're ready to give up the whole club," Johnny fumed. "No toughness. I don't get it."

"Johnny is right," Joe interrupted. "A lot of guys were joining the club just to act tough. Swagger into a bar, start fights wanting the entire club to back them up."

"A club should always back their brother," Hank added.

"Yes true, but not when they are going around acting tough simply cuz they have the Reapers patch on their backs. They should be tough, then join," Joe continued.

"Or they think the club is a way to make money. Increase their drug dealing business or whatever," Johnny added.

"What's that old JFK saying?" Joe asked. "Ask not what your country can do for you, but what you can do for your country? That goes the same for the Steel Reapers. Don't join for what the club can do for you, but for what you can do for your club."

"Well said," Johnny added.

"Not to sound like an old fart, 'You kids get off my lawn and all that,' but I almost feel like kids these days are cut from a different cloth," stated Hank.

"Oh yeah, I can see that. Don't get me wrong, there are still some cool younger guys, but on the whole... you know..." said Johnny.

"Sadly yes, I do," Hank replied.

"So I sat down, told them I was wanted out. I had done my time, ya know? Thirty-two years I think," Johnny explained. "All was good then six months later I hear I am out bad, what a bunch of BS."

"Yeah they did him dirty," Joe added. "I left shortly after Johnny. I couldn't be in the club without him."

"I get it," Hank replied. "So they made you out bad too?"

"Actually no, they didn't," Joe explained. "I guess Johnny rubbed them up the wrong way."

"Their loss," Hank said. "Johnny is one of the best fighters I have ever seen."

"Thanks old man." Johnny smiled. "That said, I have seen you knock out more cats than anyone else in the '80s."

"Those days are long behind me boys." Hank shrugged, finishing off his tacos. "Thanks for the lunch, Joe, much appreciated."

"Yeah, thanks," added Johnny. "These were damn good. Let me finish my soda, take a piss and I'll be ready to roll."

"No rush," said Hank, holding up his soda bottle which was less than halfway done.

"How much further to dog town?" asked Joe.

"Huh?" said Hank. "Oh, you mean Chihuahua?"

"Yeah," Joe replied.

"Probably about three hours, if we factor in bathroom and gas station breaks," Hank said. "We should get there just before sunset."

"Okay cool," said Joe.

Johnny returned from the bathroom. "Ready?" he asked.

"Almost bro," said Hank, holding up his bottle of coke "Gimmie a sec."

Johnny sat back down and asked Hank, "Where are we staying tonight?

"I've got a couple of rooms booked at a little hotel just off the main shopping strip, you will like it. We can park the bikes round back, so they are not seen from the street," Hank explained.

"Okay cool," Johnny replied.

They finished their lunch, and Joe grabbed their empty plates and bottles and returned them to the front counter and said, "Gracias," one of the few words of Spanish he knew. The lady behind the counter smiled and took the dirty plates from him.

"All set boys?" Joe asked when he returned.

"Yeah, good to go," Johnny replied, standing up and grabbing his riding gloves.

CHAPTER SEVENTEEN

The trio headed outside to their bikes. As they were firing their bikes up Joe tapped his tank.

"Hey old man, is there a gas station near here? I gotta refill," Joe asked.

Hank thought for a moment. "Yeah, there is one on the outskirts of main street. Actually, we should all top up our tanks. Follow me."

They all pulled out and followed Hank up the main route in town. Within minutes they were at a gas station.

After they all filled their tanks a short fat lady of about sixty approached them.

"Chicos, se ven cansados. Creo que necesitan descansar en mi cabaña."

"What the hell?" asked Johnny.

Hank shook his head. "You don't wanna know."

The woman stood there waiting for an answer.

Hank reached into his wallet and gave her a handful of pesos. "No, gracias señorita, tenemos que irnos. Tenemos un largo viaje por delante. Dios lo bendiga."

"What in tarnation??" asked Joe.

"Never mind fellas. Let's go," was all Hank said.

They pulled out and followed Hank back onto Highway 45 heading south towards Chihuahua.

CHAPTER EIGHTEEN

The boys made good time for about forty-five minutes before Johny started feeling the call of nature again. Fuck, he really had to stop drinking heavily the night before a run. He pulled ahead of Joe and Hank and gave the gesture that they would need to stop soon.

Hank acknowledged and waved that they should keep going. To Johnny that meant he knew of a place nearby to stop and that would work for him. He could hold it a lil longer.

Sure enough, within a couple of miles Johnny saw signs for the turn off to a town called Sueco. That would work. Hank waved at them both and gave the signal to be ready to pull off the highway. They followed him and within a few minutes, they were pulling into a gas station at the end of town.

"Really? Again?" asked Hank.

"Shut up and keep an eye on my bike, would ya?" Johnny snapped.

Hank laughed, turning to Joe as he said, "Hey, we should really gas up again."

"Sounds good," Joe replied. "But I gotta go piss too."

Hank shook his head and rolled over to the pumps to refuel his tank. He normally got about a hundred miles to the tank but so far on this run he found he was averaging about eighty miles per tank. Probably the warm weather, he assumed.

After refueling he went into the gas station to look for Johnny and Joe and found them inside trying to purchase drinks.

Good thinking, he thought and grabbed a large bottle of cold water too. Riding all day in the sun he found you could get way more dehydrated than you expected, leading to heat stroke. Which was nasty.

"We have about forty-five minutes to go after this and chances are we will hit evening rush hour traffic on our way in," he told the pair.

Joe and Johnny refueled their gas tanks in preparation for the remainder of the ride. Once they were ready everyone followed Hank back onto the highway and headed south towards Chihuahua.

They were smooth sailing for the next thirty minutes with Hank leading the way. Johnny was watching him and noticed he started waving his left hand behind his back. What sort of signal was that? It made no sense; it wasn't something they had preplanned. It looked like his gloved hand was making the "C" shape.

C? Had to mean cartel. Johnny reduced his speed a little, as did Joe. He noticed that the cars ahead of them were slowing too. *Shit, maybe this was a bad idea after all. Shot down in a hail of bullets outside of some random town deep into Mexico.*

Soon Johnny could see the reason they were slowing down. Masked men on both sides of the road with a white pick-up truck that appeared to have a fifty caliber rifle mounted in the back seat. He felt himself tense as they got closer. Despite the men wearing face masks he could feel their eyes scrutinizing them as they passed. Johnny looked ahead and saw Hank give them a small wave. One of the men nodded as they drove by. *What the fuck? Hank knows these guys?*

They cruised on. Fifteen minutes later they started seeing the signs for Chihuahua. Sure enough, a fair amount of traffic. Nothing like Phoenix at rush hour but after the last two days of traveling it seemed like a lot. They followed Hank as he led them through city streets weaving in and out of trucks and cars.

Johnny marveled at the Spanish architecture as they drove by. He was never a particularly religious man but the old Catholic churches were really impressive. He could definitely see the appeal of retiring here when it was all said and done.

Hank weaved to the right and Johnny and Joe followed his lead as he drove up the curb and down the side of a cobble stone alley way into a courtyard.

Hank pulled off his helmet and announced, "We're here."

"Wow! Not bad," exclaimed Joe.

"Will our bikes be safe in this courtyard?" asked Johnny.

"Yeah, I think so. I've stayed here before and there is someone on site twenty-four seven. Besides, we are down an alley, nothing is gonna be seen from the street," Hank explained.

They grabbed their gear and followed Hank to the front office to check in. Hank had come through again for the guys. They soon found their respective rooms and dumped their bags.

"Wanna meet out here in fifteen minutes and we will go grab food?" asked Hank.

"Sure," Johnny replied, nodding at Joe to make sure it was okay with him.

"Works for me," Joe added.

The bikers met up after everyone had checked into their rooms and freshened up.

Johnny exited his room to see Hank waiting for them in the courtyard.

"We riding or walking, old man?" asked Johnny.

"Walking Ace, no need to bring any gear with ya," Hank explained.

"Okay cool." Johnny dropped his helmet and gloves back into his room and re-locked his hotel door.

Moments later Joe appeared with his riding gear too. "You won't need it bro. We are walking," shouted Johnny.

Joe appeared moments later, and they followed Hank back out of the motel courtyard to the street. He made a couple of turns pointing out the central shopping district and took them to a hole-in-the-wall Steakhouse.

"This place does great Filet Mignon," explained Hank.

"It's about your turn to buy, isn't it?" asked Joe.

To his surprise the waitress handed them all menus in English and Spanish. *Okay good,* thought Johnny, *one less thing to worry about.*

He skimmed the menu for Filet Mignon which sounded good right about now. 122 dollars for a steak? He had heard that the steaks in this region were meant to be top notch but over 100 dollars? Forget it. He could get a great Filet Mignon in Phoenix for around forty-five!

"One hundred and twenty-two dollars for a steak? Screw that," Johnny swore.

Hank laughed.

"What's so funny, old man?" asked Johnny.

"Most places here say dollars. They mean Mexican dollars, meaning pesos. That steak is literally... oh six dollars!" Hank explained.

"Wait what? Six dollars for filet mignon? Are you serious?" Joe asked incredulously.

"Deadly serious," Hank replied.

"Oh shit–dinner on me tonight boys!" Johnny laughed.

"I could get used to this," remarked Joe.

CHAPTER NINETEEN

The trio sipped on red wine as they waited for their food to arrive.

"So what was up with those masked men and that fifty caliber mounted on the back of that pick-up truck?" asked Johnny. "Cartel right?"

"Noooo, federales," Hank replied.

"You mean like the feds?" asked Joe.

"Yeah, like the feds," Hank explained. "Most of them wear masks to stop the gangsters from figuring out their identities and hurting their families."

"Wow, is there much of that down here?" asked Joe.

"Nah, not really. However, a few years back a Rival Cartel showed up here and caused havoc. Eventually everything was sorted, so the feds just like to come here every now and then to flex their muscles and help keep the peace," Hank explained.

"Ah, ok. Cool," Joe replied.

"So lemme ask," said Johnny, "with a heavy federales presence on the highways do you think it's wise for us to mule all that coke back to the USA?"

"Oh yeah definitely." Hank smiled. "Once we leave Mazatlan we will be taking a lot of back roads that run parallel to the highways. We will be just fine."

"Ok cool, thanks Hank. Had to ask, ya know?" Johnny replied.

"Yeah, I get it."

Their steaks came and they were as good as any high-end steak house in Phoenix but at a fraction of the price. Johnny was seriously impressed. He could see how Hank had ended up living here, especially if you were an old dude on a tight budget.

After dinner Hank ordered them a carafe of Sangria and made excuses to go and make some phone calls. He walked outside to make his calls and Johnny turned to Joe.

"Joe, so what was up with him waving at those feds?" asked Johnny.

"He was probably just trying to fly under the radar, ya know?' Joe explained. "Like no point in giving them the evil eye, probably cause us a whole heap of hassle, if he did."

"You don't think he's working with them?" asked Johnny.

"Nah, hell. now Hank is OG, he wouldn't get in bed with the cops," Joe replied.

"Original gangster or not people do change, especially when they get older," said Johnny.

"I think he's cool Ace," Joe replied.

"Okay then. What about that lady he was talking to earlier?" asked Johnny.

"What lady?" Joe questioned.

"The one where we stopped for lunch! Villa Akihabara or whatever it was called."

'The waitress?" asked Joe.

"No, no. After lunch we stopped for gas and an old lady approached us. He said something to her in Spanish and then brushed it off like it was nothing," Johnny replied.

"She was probably asking for spare change or something," Joe replied. "I wouldn't worry about it. Truth be told I had totally forgotten about her."

"You see that's your problem brother. You are far too trusting." Johnny came back with, "Ya gotta be more suspicious if you want to survive in this game."

Joe looked at Johnny sideways. "Okay, I will try and keep that in mind

Hank returned. "All good boys?" he asked the pair.

"Yeah, all good," Joe replied. "I was just wondering about that old lady you were talking to earlier."

"Which old lady?" asked Hank, somewhat confused.

"The one at the gas station," Joe confirmed.

"Oh, that one! Ah, she was just asking us for money. I told her sorry, no." Hank shrugged.

"I figured as much," said Joe, looking at Johnny with a *"I told you so"* look on his face.

Johnny paid the bill, and the trio left the steakhouse. They walked back towards the motel until Hank led them past the turn off.

"Let's grab a quick drink before we turn in for the night," he suggested.

"Cool, let's do it," Joe replied.

Johnny and Joe grabbed a table in the small bar as old man Hank went to get them beers. These days Johnny preferred bars like this where the music was quiet, and you could have a conversation without having to strain your vocal chords.

CHAPTER TWENTY

Hank brought three beers over to their table and passed on to both Joe and Johnny before sitting down.

"Cheers brothers, it's been so good to catch up. I've missed this," he said, raising his bottle.

Joe and Johnny followed suit and raised their beers to their newly reconnected brotherhood.

Hank started talking about some of the old faces and what became of them.

"How did that English guy work out? Steven Atwell?" asked Hank.

"Simon," Joe corrected him.

"Ah, yeah Simon, he was a character," Hank said. "I liked him."

"Ha!" commented Johnny. "Atwell? More like RATwell!"

"Oh shit, what happened? He had just made full patch when I left Arizona for Mexico," hank explained.

"Well, he had a big ecstasy ring–supplying all the ASU college kids with their party favors," explained Johnny.

"He was making bank and brought in some of the club to share the wealth and expand the operation."

"Okay..." said Hank, waiting for the inevitable shoe to drop.

"So somewhere along the line he gets popped," Johnny explained. "Joe reckons more than likely one of the college kid street level dealers he recruited got caught. The kid flips on Simon and Simon tries to save himself by ratting on the club brothers who were brought into the ring by him."

"Pure scumbag move," Joe commented.

Hank nodded in agreement. "Weak sauce."

"Yeah, but it gets better," Johnny hastily added.

"Let me guess, they all go to prison, and he runs off back to the UK?" guessed Hank.

"Nope, better than that." Joe smiled.

"Oh okay... I'm listening," Hank replied, swigging on his beer, wondering where this was all heading.

"Remember the Victorville Biker Massacre?" asked Johnny.

"Yeah, that was after I had left the club," said Hank. "But I remember."

"Ten killed, 177 arrested," Joe added.

"What happened to everyone arrested?' asked Hank. "Lengthy prison sentences I'm sure."

"Wait wait, you're jumping ahead," Johnny scolded.

"Okay then hurry up and tell us what happened to English Simon?" asked Hank.

"So he was one of the ten killed," Johnny said with a smile on his face. "Karma, right?"

"Yeah—justice for once," added Joe.

"Wow that's crazy," Hank exclaimed. "So what happened to everyone else?"

"After a long and drawn-out court case all charges were dropped against our brothers who were arrested," Johnny replied.

"Get out, that never happens," said Hank rather surprised.

"Well, it did this time." Johnny smiled.

"And what about the guys from the Lost Wolves club?" asked Hank. "They all got time behind the wire?"

"Nope, they were let off too," Johnny explained.

"What am I missing here?" asked Hank. "The police must have messed up big time with their evidence gathering."

"You could say that," Joe said. "So get this..."

"I'm ready," said Hank.

"All of the casings they found..." Joe paused for dramatic effect, "were from the cops' rifles. Our guys didn't fire a damn shot. Not one."

"Are you serious? That's out and out murder," fumed Hank.

"Of course it is," said Johnny, shaking his head. "As far as I am aware not one cop got put on trial."

"That's such bullshit," Hank responded.

"Yeah, it is," Joe replied. "There are theories that perhaps it was done to silence RATwell."

"Yeah, could be. That's not really a stretch to imagine," Hank replied. "Especially in this day and age."

CHAPTER TWENTY-ONE

Joe looked over and could see nearly everyone was done with their beers. Without asking he got up and headed to the bar to buy another round. He was feeling pretty good and didn't want their fun to stop. He returned with three beers of which he handed one to Hank and the other to Johnny.

"Here ya go boys, my round."

"Thanks Joe," said Hank. "I gotta piss, be right back."

Old man Hank got up and headed to the back of the small bar in search of the restrooms.

Johnny turned to Joe.

"You see that?" he asked.

"See what?" said Joe, slightly confused.

"He asked about RATwell," Johnny hissed.

"So? So what?" asked Joe, still confused.

"He's testing us cuz he knows we know he's a rat," Johnny explained.

"Dude c'mon! It's old man Hank. He ain't no rat," Joe said, puzzled as to how Johnny could make such a leap in logic.

"You're wrong, brother, you're fucking wrong," Johnny replied, then clammed up as Hank returned to their table.

"Everything alright boys?" he asked, almost as if he could feel the tension in the air.

"Yeah, all hunky dory here," Joe replied, raising his bottle of beer to Hank and then to Johnny.

"Okay good," Hank replied, swigging from his bottle of beer.

Trying to change the subject and relieve the tension, Joe asked Hank, "So what's tomorrows ride?"

"We are heading to Durango," Hank explained. "Probably about eight hours riding I reckon."

"Sounds good," Joe replied.

"I've only done that road once but from memory there are a lot of twists and turns," Hank said. "So you know what it's like. Ride your own ride."

"Oh like that's it?" asked Johnny.

"Yeah, there are some gas stations and small towns in between but if one of us crashes in the middle of nowhere it's not gonna end well," Hank replied. "You know what I'm saying."

"I get the idea," Johnny replied.

"If we get separated, I suggest we all pull over and wait at the very next gas station," Hank suggested.

"Works for me," said Joe, nodding his head in agreement.

"Agreed," said Johnny, nodding his head.

They finished Joe's beers and Johnny got up to buy a round for everyone. He wasn't planning to drink this much tonight as he knew he would be back and forth to the bathroom all night long but considering both Hank and Joe had bought beers, it was the right thing to do. He would deal with the consequences once he got back to their hotel.

CHAPTER TWENTY-TWO

Sure enough, every hour throughout the entire night Johnny was up and hitting the bathroom to empty his bladder. Was he this bad when he was twenty-one? He couldn't remember. He probably would have slept through it and pissed his jeans back in those days.

Of course, by 7 a.m., he was just settling into a deep sleep when Joe banged on his hotel room door.

"Hey man, we're just going to go grab breakfast if you wanna join us," he shouted.

Fuck, I need to rest, thought Johnny.

"No man, I'm gonna grab a little more shut eye. Grab me when you get back," he groaned. It was going to be a long, sleep deprived day.

"Will do," Joe replied, no doubt going to grab old man Hank.

To Johnny's surprise, he actually fell back into a deep sleep. When Joe knocked on the door again, he was confused for a moment. *Where am I? Who is waking me up from this glorious sleep I was having?*

"Hey sleepy head, come on, time to go. Hands off cocks, hands on socks. Get dressed ya bastard," Joe shouted through the door.

"Goddamm, alright already. Gimmie ten minutes," Johnny groaned. He could have slept for the rest of the day. Hopefully, they didn't have a long ride today.

Johnny got up, took a piss, brushed his teeth. Dressed and packed his gear. Then he had to piss again. Damn he really had to stop drinking so much on this run. He could see himself pissing for the rest of the day at this rate. No good.

He checked out of the room and headed to the lobby to return the remote. Apparently in some of these hotels people walked away with the remotes for the TV so you had to return it to ensure you got your refund. Weird, but whatever.

He walked out to the car park to secure his gear to his bike only to be greeted by Hank and Joe laughing.

"Oh look it's sleeping beauty," joked Hank.

"Yeah, yeah. Whatever," Johnny grumbled.

"Long one today boys," Hank replied. "Remember there's a part where there are lots of twisties so bring your A game."

"Oh yeah, that's right," said Joe. "Now I remember you telling us last night."

Hank dummy checked his bike to make sure nothing had come loose after yesterday's ride.

"We should gas up on the way out of town boys," Hank suggested. "Everyone ready?"

Johnny wasn't ready, in fact he could already tell it was going to be a long and painful day of riding. He was already feeling sleep deprived. "Yeah, I'm good to go," he lied.

"I'm good too," Joe added.

They pulled out of the motel courtyard and followed Hank down their side street to the main road. He soon located a gas station on the way out of town and they topped up their tanks. Johnny ran into the store to get himself a fountain soda to hydrate before the long ride. He pounded his beverage and tossed the cup into the trash.

"Alright I am ready! Let's ride guys," he announced.

Hank pulled his helmet back on, looked to see if Joe was ready and fired up his scoot for the first leg of their long ride today. He led them out of town and back onto the highway heading south towards Durango.

The first fifty miles or so out of Chihuahua could be any stretch of road in Arizona Johnny felt. They passed through small towns that looked like they had seen better days. Sure enough, about an hour in Johnny felt the call of nature. He pulled in front of Hank and gave "the signal". Hank nodded and pointed to the soft shoulder ahead. Apparently, there were no towns nearby worth stopping in.

"Let me guess, ya gotta go already?" asked Hank, slightly teasing.

"I told you before," Johnny replied, "when I drink I gotta piss, so sue me."

He jumped off his bike and went to find a place to piss where he wouldn't be bitten by any snakes lurking in the scrub.

He returned to hear Joe talking to Hank.

"Sure is some amazing countryside down this way," Joe commented.

"Definitely." Hank smiled. "I love this part of the world."

"You good now bro?" Joe asked Johnny.

"Yeah, good for now, let's get going. I am keen to hit these twisties the old man keeps threatening us with," Johnny replied.

"Hey man, just ride your own ride. No sense in stacking it in the middle of nowhere Ace," Hank replied.

They fired up their scoots, let them idle for a moment, turned to make sure they were clear to go and pulled back on to the highway heading south. Hank led the way with Johnny following close behind and Joe behind him in a staggered formation. Hank and Joe kept closest to the shoulder with Johnny near the dividing line for the traffic heading north. Years of discipline in club runs helped them stay in position as they roared down the highway towards Durango.

Soon enough they were hitting the twisties that Hank had warned them of. A sharp right, followed by a sharp left, then a right again. Johnny felt his pegs drag on one right turn. He was sure Joe would have witnessed sparks if he was watching. This whole stretch of road demanded that every fiber of Johnny's body stay alert and focused. Twist throttle, counter steer, roll off the throttle, squeeze the clutch, change gears, release, twist throttle and repeat. It was a master class in riding skills and at times Johnny felt his back wheel start to lose grip on one particular sharp turn. The rubber only grabbed the pavement at the last moment. Hank was right. You did not want to wreck it out here. A death sentence, surely.

Some of the views were awe inspiring. It reminded Johnny of some of the roads he had travelled on in Northern Arizona. Majestic mountain ranges and deserted valleys as far as the eye could see.

The road went on and on. Johnny was starting to lose focus. He swore at one moment he was temporarily asleep. Just for a moment, but enough to scare him. The last few nights of minimum sleep and long rides were taxing him. Big time. He had to face it he was no longer in his wild and carefree twenties. There were times where he and the club would have been able to ride twelve, fourteen hours at a stretch without issue. He was old. He needed to rest.

Just as he was about to suggest to Hank that they take a break the old man started signaling that they would soon be pulling over. Johnny checked a road sign: "Torreon". Never heard of it, but he was glad they were stopping. He needed food, he needed to hydrate. He needed a break before he fell asleep on his hog and rode off a mountain top.

Joe and Johnny followed Hank closely as he weaved through the streets of Torreon. Johnny never knew this town existed, but he had to admire the architecture in the central business district. Very nice. He was all about it. Old school Spanish, colonial style. It seemed to him that Torreon was a city of two halves. The haves and the have nots. Then again, wasn't every city filled with those with not much and those with too much?

Hank rode a block or two past the huge fountains in the central square with Johnny and Joe following close behind. If they lost him now, they would be screwed. It was one thing to pull up along the side of a lonely highway and be spotted by your brothers but in a busy downtown area like this they could be lost for hours.

Finally, Hank seemed to find what he was looking for and gave the guys the signal to park up. They followed his lead and backed their bikes up against the curb.

"You boys hungry?" asked Hank. "I know you gotta be Johnny. Ya missed breakfast."

"Yeah, I'm starving," Johnny replied. "So, what's so great about this place?"

"Eh, I've eaten here before I can vouch for their food," Hank explained. "Trust me, get the birria combo. It's insanely good."

"I'll take your word for it, old man" Joe commented, eyeing the pictures on the menu.

Johnny and Joe grabbed some seats towards the back of the small restaurant and Hank went up to order, since he was the most fluent in Spanish.

"You need some money for this?" asked Johnny when Hank returned with a couple of bottles of soda.

"Sure man. Twelve bucks should cover it, thanks."

"Well, I can see why you warned us on those twisties," Joe remarked. "I nearly slid out once or twice there."

"Haha, me too." Johnny laughed.

"See, I warned ya," Hank replied.

The waitress arrived with three trays of tacos and a cup of what looked like a dark soup for each of them.

"Soup?" asked Joe.

"Nah, it's like a dipping sauce. Dip 'em in and take a bite. Trust me on this," Hank explained.

Joe and Johnny dug in.

"Damn this is some good shit," Johnny remarked.

"See, I told ya." Hank laughed, devouring his food.

Within minutes Johnny had finished his meal. He almost had to slow his pace while eating. He wasn't sure if he was just starving after skipping breakfast or whether the food was so good. He basically inhaled it. He looked over and Joe had pretty much down the same thing.

"Wow, that was damn good," Joe commented.

"By far the best food we have had on this run," Johnny added.

"Hey old man, how much further do we have to get to Durango?" asked Joe.

"Hmm with the amount of rest stops you two need I would guess another four hours or so, eh maybe three."

Johnny sat and let his food digest and swigged on his bottle of coke, finishing it off.

"Alright, let me take a piss and let's get back on the road."

"Sounds good," said Joe, grabbing their trays and returning them to the front counter.

When Johnny met Hank and Joe outside, they both had their necks turned and were looking to the North.

"What's going on?" asked Johnny.

"Hank was just checking those storm clouds headed our way," Joe explained. "We are gonna have to haul ass to avoid getting stuck in that fucker."

Johnny looked up and saw the ominous black and gray clouds rapidly coming in.

"Oh shit, let's go, NOW," he said, slinging on his backpack and pulling on his helmet.

The pair followed old man Hank as he weaved through the afternoon traffic to find the on ramp for the 400 Highway south. Within minutes they were back on the blacktop and moving out. Nothing more miserable than being stuck in torrential rain, your clothes soaked and trying to not slide out on your scoot.

About an hour into this leg of their journey, Johnny felt the need to piss again. Fuck, what to do. Pull over and risk getting soaked, or keep riding and piss his jeans? He dared to check his rear-view mirrors and felt like they had enough time to make a quick stop. He pulled ahead of Hank and waved at him. Hank nodded and they found a hard shoulder to pull over on.

Hank pulled off his helmet and shouted at Johnny, "Better hurry son or we are all gonna be soaked to the skin," said the old man.

At that point Joe decided it was probably best to take a piss too and found a bush close enough to Johnny but not too close to make it awkward so he could relieve himself too.

Relieved, Johnny scrambled back to his bike and shouted at Joe.

"Ya got thirty seconds and we are gonna leave your ass behind."

"Fuck you guys," yelled Joe, semi joking.

He ran back to his bike, pulling up his zipper and tightening his belt as he moved. He leapt on his bike and dared to look back at the looming storm clouds.

"Let's goo!" he shouted as he pulled out, off the shoulder and back down the highway. They were going to have to gun it to outrun the rainstorms that were bearing down on them.

Luckily for the trio there were not too many cars on the road. They rode hard and fast, traffic cops be damned. Actually, Johnny didn't want to run into local cops as he imagined they would either arrest them and lock them up on false charges or beat them by the side of the road and leave them lying in a pool of their own blood. Neither option appealed to him right now. He was hoping the local law enforcement boys were in a nice dry café somewhere right now drinking coffee or sipping on a beer. All he wanted to do was get to Durango nice and dry.

Despite a couple of delays clearing tolls booths, which seemed to be everywhere on Mexican highways, the boys made fast work of the stretch of highway between Torreon and Durango. To Johnny's surprise they were soon seeing road signs for the rapidly approaching Durango. Checking his rear-view mirrors, Johnny could see the gray storm clouds were still on their tail.

Had they actually done it? Ridden out the storm? They slowed to take the exit ramp into Durango and Johnny felt a few droplets hit his jeans. They probably had minutes before the heavens opened up on them. He prayed that whatever arrangements Hank had made for accommodations for the night were not too far away.

They weaved through rush hour traffic staying as close to Hank as possible without running into him. With the quick glimpses afforded to him Johnny felt Durango could be any mid-sized mid-western city in the United States, except with everything in Spanish.

The clouds started to spit. He noticed dark droplets forming on his worn jeans. Hank raced ahead the moment the next traffic light turned green. Joe and Johnny followed tightly. Hank signaled a right turn, and they followed him down the smaller side street. Less pedestrians on the street now, no doubt safely ensconced inside and not because the street was historically in a desolate part of town. Hank gestured wildly. "Left turn ahead!" They were out of time. He could feel the rain hitting his helmet and jacket now.

After making their left turn Hank waved to his right and started to reduce speed. Up ahead Johnny saw the unmistakable neon sign for a hotel. Not a moment too soon.

They entered the courtyard for the hotel and the skies opened up. Torrential rains came pounding down. They just had enough time to jump off their bikes and grab their gear, taking shelter in the hotel's courtyard. They stood there for a moment watching the flood of water come down before turning and heading inside the hotel.

After checking in they decided to go to their rooms and chill out for thirty minutes before hitting the streets in search of food. Johnny noticed his room was next door to Hank's with Joe's down the hall on the same floor.

Johnny dumped his bags on the bed and returned to the hallway to follow the sign he had noticed earlier for a vending machine. He continued down to the end of the hall and there were two vending machines shoved in an alcove off the hallway. He grabbed two bags of potato chips from one and two bottles of water from the other vending machine. Returning to his room, he pulled off his boots and socks and sat on his bed. Despite the stormy weather he was hot and sweaty. *Fuck it,* he thought, *I'll have a quick shower before heading out.*

After showering, Johnny sat on his bed. It was only then it dawned on him just how physically exhausted he was. The days of hard riding had taken its toll on his aging body. *Shit, I should probably stay in tonight and skip dinner and drinks,* he realized. He grabbed the TV's remote and tried to find something mindless to watch while he waited on Joe and Hank.

While flicking through the channels he could hear a phone somewhere nearby making the noise of a "face time call." *Shit, that's coming from Hank's room,* he realized. He put his ear against the wall and strained to hear the conversation. He could hear Hank announcing, "Hey, it's me," and after that he could hear more talking but couldn't make out a word he was saying. Now more than ever he was convinced that Hank had something to hide. *What though?*

118

As he lay there wondering what Hank's game was, he heard a light *tap tap tap* at his door. Must be Joe, he thought. He pulled on his boxers and answered the door. Sure enough, it was Joe.

"Hey brother, you nearly ready?" asked Joe, all smiles.

"Come in, come in," Johnny gestured, closing the hotel room door the moment Joe stepped inside.

"What's up?" asked Joe curiously.

He dragged Joe into the bathroom, the furthest point away from the shared wall to Hank's room.

"You okay brother?" asked Joe, confused.

"Hey," whispered Johnny. "I heard Hank making a face time call a few minutes ago."

"A face time what?" asked Joe. "Ah a face time call. Okay, so?"

"Who the hell is he talking to?" asked Johnny. "Has to be the feds!"

"What? No! It's probably his kids, man," Joe countered. "Geez."

"Does he have kids?" asked Johnny. "I didn't think he did."

"Everyone's got kids bro, ya gotta chill," Joe replied. "Anyways, we are gonna go out and get some food and beers, pull your jeans on."

Johnny looked out the window. The rain was still coming down hard.

"Eh, I reckon I am gonna stay in brother," Johnny replied. "I'm exhausted and need an early night."

"Oh c'mon! I've never known Ace McIntire to turn down food and drink. Just come out and you'll have a good time," Joe replied.

"Nah. I've made my mind up, gonna just chill brother. You and the old man go," Joe looked deflated. "You sure bro? C'mon!"

"Nah, I'm sure. Thanks though," Johnny replied. "Just keep an eye on that old fuck, would ya?"

"Yeah, sure Johnny, sure," said Joe, heading for the front door. "Last chance?"

"Nah. I'm just gonna rest up. See you in the morning." Johnny closed the door behind Joe after he exited the room.

He could hear Joe knocking on Hank's door through the front door of his room. He listened for a moment as Hank let him in and jumped back on his bed and continued his search for a TV show to watch.

CHAPTER TWENTY-THREE

Johnny settled on a re-run of an episode of the Charlie Sheen comedy show, *Two and A Half Men* dubbed in Spanish but he remembered the episode and laughed along regardless. He ate his potato chips for dinner and washed it down with one of his bottles of water. Soon enough Johnny was fighting to stay awake and ended up flicking off the TV set and passing out.

He woke up as the first rays of sunshine peaked over the horizon. He had managed to sleep all night without hitting the bathroom. A rarity for him. He struggled to get out of bed, his back and hips super tight and twisted. He hit the bathroom, did his thing, brushed his teeth and drank the other bottle of water.

What now? Get dressed? Go get breakfast? Wake the other guys up? He struggled to recall if they had set a time last night to meet up. Chances were, knowing those two reprobates, they got in drunk and very late and were still asleep. He decided to jump back into bed and flick on the TV set. He was sure that Joe would be along soon enough wanting to go eat breakfast.

More than an hour had passed since Johnny had woken up. Still nothing, Shit, he didn't even think he knew what room Joe was in. (He knew Hank's as it was right next door). Should he go wake Hank or keep waiting? He was definitely hungry now. Probably the first time since they left Phoenix that he actually wanted breakfast, and Joe was a no show. *Was it like this when they were waiting on him?* He imagined so.

Just as Johnny was contemplating venturing out on his own to seek out breakfast options, he heard a light tapping on his hotel room door. He walked to the door and asked, "Yeah?"

"Hey brother, it's Joe, we're gonna head out in five minutes and get some breakfast. You wanna come with us?" Joe asked.

"Oh hell yeah, I'm starving. Meet you in the lobby in five," Johnny replied.

After meeting in the lobby, the trio headed out in search of a decent breakfast spot.

"You get any rest Ace?" Hank asked Johnny.

"Yeah, I passed out about ten minutes after Joe swung by my room," Johnny explained. "How was last night?"

"Ugh, I'm hurting big time," Joe bemoaned. "I might have to do your trick from here on out."

Johnny laughed. "Yeah, right."

They found a local breakfast spot, again with no menus in English, so Hank had to order for everyone.

"What do you want?" he asked Joe and Johnny.

"That Jose ranchero thing," Joe asked,

"Yeah, me too," Johnny added.

"Oh you mean Huevos Rancheros?" Hank laughed. "Before you guys leave this country I want you at least being able to order properly."

The waitress bought over their coffee orders and some bottled water for Hank and Joe who were definitely feeling it today. Johnny was somewhat amused. It actually felt great not to be hungover and sleep deprived for once. Maybe there was something in these guys who preached the sober lifestyle after all?

Johnny sipped on his coffee. *Damn, this is great coffee!* Waayyy better than anything he'd had in the USA.

"Damn, great coffee boys," Johnny stated.

"Yeah. I think you missed out the last two days, sleeping in and all," Joe teased.

"Yeah, yeah. Whatever," Johnny replied. "So Hank, what's the plan for the day?"

"We are heading to Mazatlan," Hank explained.

"Where's that?" asked Joe.

Hank thought for a moment. "Southwest of here. Approximately a four-hour ride."

"Not bad," Joe replied.

"However," Hank added.

"There's always a however," Johnny interrupted.

"Yeah, well. Let me finish," Hank continued. "We have to stop at a small town just before Mazatlan called Copala first."

"Why do we have to do that?" asked Johnny.

"We pay there, they make the call to Mazatlan and we pick up there," Hank explained.

"Wait, what?" Johnny shouted. "We leave our money with one guy we don't know from Adam and then carry on our merry way with the hope that we don't get stiffed down the road?"

"Look, I know it sounds bizarre but it's their house, their rules. Think of the old school street level drug dealers. You pay them and once they verify the money, they usually have a friend half way down the block holding who gives you the drugs."

"Yeah, I get it," said Joe. "What do you call it? Mitigate your losses?"

"Yeah, something like that," Hank replied.

"Well, I don't like it bro. Who's to say we don't get ripped off?" asked Johnny.

"Well, me, for one," said Hank. "I have vouched for you guys, and I have vouched for them. It's gonna be fine Ace. Trust me."

"I don't, I just don't know," Johnny grumbled.

"Look Ace. We are old school. Our word is our bond. That's our brotherhood. Without our word, what do we have? Nothing!"

Internally, Johnny was mad. He didn't like this at all. He felt Hank had put him in a bad position with this arrangement. But too late to back out now. He just had to roll with it and have faith it would work out for him.

The waitress bought over their breakfasts and they all tucked in. Johnny loosened up a bit. The tasty food put him into a better state of mind. But he still wasn't happy. It just felt wrong. All wrong.

CHAPTER TWENTY-FOUR

S o a couple more things you need to know…" Hank started.

Oh god what now? thought Johnny.

"Here we go, what else?" asked Johnny.

"We will be officially entering cartel country. If we do get stopped or questioned let me do all the talking. Trust me, we don't want to start anything with these guys. Some of them are little guys of a slight build. But you fight one, we take on all of them. They are the type they will kill us and then go and hunt down every one of our family members no matter where they are in the world and kill them too. Just to make a point. So do not start shit," Hank explained.

"Well sorry old man. If they start on me, I'm not backing down. Fuck that," Johnny replied.

"Yeah, I understand what you're saying, Ace, you're OG, but just follow my lead okay?" said Hank.

Joe was starting to look worried

"Okay, so anything else?" he asked.

"Yeah, now that you mention it," Hank replied. "The road we are riding on today is called El Espinazo Del Diablo."

"Okay, what the hell is that supposed to mean?" asked Johnny. "You know damn well we don't speak any Spanish."

"It means the Devil's Backbone," explained Hank. "Lots of Twisties on this leg, so stay frosty. Ride your own ride. Some steep drops if you low side and... I'm not even kidding. Some stretches there are just cattle, like Oxen or whatever just wandering around. You hit one of them going sixty and guess who is gonna come out of it worse off?"

"Oh boy," Johnny said. "Are you kidding?"

"Nah, not kidding Ace," Hank replied.

"Unreal," swore Joe. "So how long the ride to Copala?"

Hank thought for a minute. "Hmm I would say about three hours to Copala. We stop, meet the connect, do our thing, then say fifty minutes to Mazatlan."

"Not bad," Joe replied. "I can deal with that,"

The waitress arrived with the check. Johnny handed it to Hank to explain how much it was, and Johnny took upon himself to pay. Money well spent in his opinion.

The trio finished their coffee and walked back to their hotel to check out and to start the day's journey.

They all met back in the lobby after thirty minutes of returning to their rooms. They grabbed their gear, gave their scoots a quick once over to make sure nothing had shaken loose on their last run to Durango.

Soon as they were all good, they fired up their bikes and just stood back and listened to them rumble; the sound was glorious to Johnny's ears. After letting their bikes warm up, they were good to go, following Hank back out on to the streets of Durango and weaving through the morning's traffic back onto the highway running south into the notorious Sinaloa countryside.

After a while Johnny could feel the change in elevation. They were starting to climb now. Sure enough, just as Hank had warned them soon there were plenty of twisties, long flowing turns to the right and then to the left. Some turns were pretty drastic too. Johnny rolled off the throttle and started to take it a little slower. Again, as Hank warned them, if you low slide here you are going over the edge and by the looks of it, it was a long way down. What was that old saying? "It's not the fall that kills you. It's the sudden stop at the bottom." That phrase definitely sprang to mind as Johnny followed Hank's lead around the multiple twists and turns.

On occasion they passed other riders heading the other way, and without knowing who they were, they all gave them the international riders wave with their left hands. Something car drivers would never understand.

As they continued along this treacherous but beautiful stretch of road, Johnny felt like he was high. *What gives? He didn't drink last night.* Then it dawned on him. *It was the altitude.* They were way, way up from sea level now.

Two hours into their run and Johnny was amazed he hadn't had to stop for a bathroom break. Amazing what happened when he didn't drink a bunch of beers the night before. He would have to point that out to Hank when they pulled into this town called Copala.

After a few more twists and turns, Hank started waving and pointing. They followed him as he pulled off the highway and they headed to a beautiful little town. Streets paved in cobblestones, vibrant houses in bold hues and a historic church. Johnny was digging the vibe of the place.

Hank waved again and they took a left turn down a quiet side street. Soon he was pointing to a nondescript suburban house on the right. They followed his lead and parked up by the side of the road.

This is the place? thought Johnny. *Doesn't look like something Pablo Escobar would own, but hey, whatever.*

As they pulled off their helmets, Johnny shouted over to Hank.

"Ya see? No beers, no bathroom breaks. I told ya!"

Hank looked Johnny up and down. "Yeah well, I would still go get checked out when you get back to Phoenix brother."

"Our scoots going to be safe here, old man?" Joe asked Hank.

Hank looked up and down the street. "Yeah, I think so bro."

"So, what happens now?" asked Joe.

"We're going in. I'll introduce to Momo and we do the deal," Hank explained.

"There's a guy called Momo?" asked Johnny incredulously.

"Yeah, that's his name. What of it?" Hank replied.

"I dunno, weird name for a man if you ask me," Johnny replied.

"Okay well, there ya go Ace," Hank said. "Anyways, just follow my lead and don't act the fool, alright?"

"Yeah, fine," huffed Johnny, following Hank to the front door of the small suburban home.

Chapter Twenty-Four

Hank knocked on the front door and waited. A small Hispanic woman opened the door, greeted him and eyed Johnny and Joe up and down suspiciously. The first thing that sprung to Johnny's mind was the chainsaw scene from *Scarface*. He told himself he wouldn't let his guard down for a moment when he got inside.

The woman beckoned them all to come in and Johnny and Joe dumped their backpacks in the hallway just past the front door before following Hank and the lady to a room in the back.

They entered what appeared to be the kitchen with a small, slightly built man sitting at a table cradling a beer.

"Heyyy, senor Hank, hola," the man greeted Hank.

Johnny assumed this must be the aforementioned Momo.

The apparent old friends hugged and he rushed to greet Joe and Johnny.

"Hola hombres, I am Momo," he said in broken English. "Beer?"

"Sure, thanks," Joe replied.

"None for me, thanks. Maybe a soda if you have one?" Johnny replied.

Momo said something to the woman in Spanish. Too fast for Johnny to pick out any words of note and she went to the fridge returning with three beers and one glass bottle of Coca-Cola. She handed them out to the men and left the room.

"Come, come." Momo gestured to another room in the house.

They walked into what appeared to be a dimly lit living room, with a couple of couches and a TV in the corner.

Hank and Momo exchanged some talk in very fluent Spanish. They could have been calling Joe and Johnny dipshits for all Johnny knew. He was hoping he could at least pick out key words here and there. Finally, he turned to Johnny and Joe with a very serious look on his face. In broken English, he said, "I am very sorry my friends. I know you're good people according to Senor Hank, but the best I can do for you is 100 dollars, American money, per kilo. Will this be acceptable?"

Johnny ran the numbers in his head. *A hundred dollars a key for sale in Arizona for 20,000 dollars? Would that be acceptable? Of course it would.*

Johnny nodded and tried not to show any look of joy on his face.

"Yes, yes, that's very kind of you. Thank you," he replied to Momo.

"Yes, thank you. A very good price Mister Momo," Joe added.

"How many kilos would you each want to purchase Senor?" asked Momo.

"Uhh would twenty each be okay?" asked Johnny.

"Of course, senor. Anything for Hank's friends." Momo nodded.

'Thank you" said Joe to their newly found friend.

"Very well then," Momo replied.

He got up and left the room and returned a few moments later with a package that was about the size of grocery store bag of flour.

"Please have a sample on me." He poured out a small mountain of white powder and started chopping it up into giant size lines. He pulled out a gold-plated coke straw and handed it to old man Hank.

"Are you kidding me? If I do that I will die. My goddam heart will explode. I will stick to beers boys."

Hank handed the straw to Johnny.

"That's all you Ace," he said.

Johnny grabbed the straw and tried to figure out which line to snort. It had been at least a good five years since Johnny had done any blow, although in the '90s it was pretty much an every weekend thing for him.

Johnny wanted to make sure he didn't make a mess knocking the other lines out of shape when he did his. The last thing he wanted to look like was an amateur.

He managed half the line. The blast of pure cocaine ripped through his brain like a bullet. He thought his head was going to explode. This stuff was the real deal.

"WOOOOO!" he shouted trying to keep control of his over charged nervous system.

He passed the straw to Joe.

"Any good?" asked Joe.

"Any good?" said Johnny struggling to sound coherent. "Any good? This is the best shit I have had in my life. WOOOOOO WOOOO!"

Joe took a line. "Oh fuck," was all he managed.

He sat back up with a stupid shit-eating grin on his face. "Oh damn, you weren't kidding Ace, this stuff is insane."

Joe handed the straw back to Momo who did two lines with ease then nodded at the bikers.

"It's okay? Yeah?" he asked.

"Yeah, yeah," said Johnny with a dreamy look on his face. "Fuck yeah."

Momo passed the straw back to Johnny. "Here you go amigo."

Johnny contemplated doing another line right away. Hmm, probably best to give it a few minutes. His heart was already going 200 miles per hour.

"I'm good, here ya go Joe," he announced, passing the metal straw to Joe.

The trio sat around drinking beers and snorting cocaine with their newfound friend Momo for an hour or so before old man Hank announced it was time to go.

"You have the money for me?" asked Momo very politely.

"Oh shit, of course, of course," Johnny replied. He pulled open his wallet and counted out the American dollars for Momo.

"So what's the deal here? How does this work?" asked Joe.

"Well of course, Momo is the money guy, and they hold the goods an hour away from here. His people have offered us use of one of their houses right near the beach in Mazatlan tonight and tomorrow they will deliver your order."

"Ah ok, thanks," Joe responded. "And it will be this good?"

"Yes, yes of course," Momo replied. "You are like Hank's friends, so you are like our friends. You understand?"

"Yes, yes. I get it," said Johnny. "Don't let us down."

"You have my word, my friend. In my country our word is everything. You understand?" Momo replied.

"I understand. Thanks Momo," Johnny replied.

"Oh before you leave I have something for you. Hold on." The man jumped up and left the room. He returned with two baseball-sized packages.

"This is a gift from me to you and your friend," he said, nodding towards Joe.

Johnny opened the bag. It was a huge baseball-sized bag of coke.

"Oh boy," Johnny replied, barely concealing his smile. "Thank you my man." He tossed the second package to Joe.

"Oh shittt," said Joe, feeling the weight and the heft of the cocaine.

"You boys ready?" asked Hank.

"Well, we are now," Johnny replied with a shit-eating grin on his face.

Momo walked them to the front door and after grabbing their packs, he said something fast in Spanish to Hank. All Johnny heard was "casa."

As they were getting back on their scoots, Johnny asked Hank, "What was that all about?"

"Momo was making sure we had the address to the condo we are staying at tonight. I told him that I did," Hank explained.

"Ahh cool, how long's the ride?" Johnny asked.

"A lil over an hour," Hank explained. "Some twisties so just stay frosty."

"Yeah, yeah, I know. Ride your own ride and all that," Johnny quipped.

"You know it." Hank winked back at the surly biker.

Johnny straddled his bike. He was still high as a kite. *Shit, could he do this? Could he ride?* It had been years since he had ridden high on coke. Oh well, he was about to find out. For better or for worse. He twisted the throttle and felt the familiar rumble of his scoot. *Here goes nothing*, he thought.

Hank looked to make sure both Joe and Johnny were ready and then gave the signal. The trio slowly rolled out of the quiet street and back towards the main road in search of the highway leading them further south and west.

CHAPTER TWENTY-FIVE

The trio rolled on with tall rock cliffs to one side and sheer drops to the other side. Johnny often marveled at the first men to make these roads. Conditions must have been tough. No truck stops to pull over and grab yourself a fountain soda for these guys. Were they prisoners? Forced to blast through mountains to make life better for others? One day he would research this and find out.

At certain parts of the old winding road, they could see the new superhighway hovering over them. A testament to modern engineering. Who came up with the first plans to build these enormous bridges? The Romans, he guessed. 2000 years ago. How do you train for creating these marvels? He had no clue. Fuck, he was high.

They passed through run down and desolate villages as they headed towards the city of Mazatlan. The new highway reminded him of the original *Psycho* movie made by Alfred Hitchcock starring Anthony Perkins. Wasn't the premise his Bates Motel was down on its luck as the new highway took away weary travelers looking for a place to stay? Johnny realized his mind was roaming and he struggled to focus on the road that lay ahead of him.

After an hour they finally started to see signs for Mazatlan. Oh good, he could feel the beers he drank at Momo's residence straining his bladder. Hopefully they would reach this promised condo soon.

Hank pulled them off the highway and once again they wove through the surface streets of another Mexican city. Johnny could see the appeal. At times he felt like he was more in Southern Europe than the Americas.

They wove through more city streets and eventually Johnny saw Hank waving and pointing to the right.

They turned down a small street and Hank pulled up beside a high brick wall and a gate with a code box. He took off one of his riding gloves, checked his cell phone and punched in a number to the digital box by the side of the gate. Slowly, it swung open. He gestured for the boys to follow him in.

It was a brand-new construction, a two storey townhouse with parking in the bricked yard for approximately two to three cars. Their bikes would be safe here tonight.

"This is it eh?" asked Joe, pulling off his helmet.

"Sure is," Hank replied. "Momo said there should be steaks in the freezer and beers in the fridge. Let's go in and check it out."

"Works for me." Joe smiled.

They grabbed their gear and Hank punched in yet another code to unlock the front door and what Johnny assumed was some form of alarm system. The place was surprisingly nice especially when compared to Momo's modest home in Copala. Johnny could see a place like this fitting in some trendy neighborhood in Old Town Scottsdale or Tempe.

They did a walkthrough of the place and found that there were three master bedrooms all with their own private shower and bathroom. A stairwell led to a roof top terrace where they could see the Ocean. Johnny didn't impress easily but he could see the appeal of retiring and living out the rest of his days in a place like this.

After choosing their respective bedrooms for the night, Johnny showered and joined the others in the kitchen where Hank had beers on the go and some burgers grilling. Joe passed Johnny a beer as he joined them.

"Nice place, eh?" asked Joe.

"Yeah, very impressive," Johnny replied. "So, his guys will arrive in the morning with the delivery?"

"Yeah, they will be here. Don't stress it bro," Hank replied.

Hank finished grilling and passed burgers to Joe and Johnny. They had just finished them off when a buzzer went off.

Oh shit, thought Johnny, *this is it, they have come to kill us after all. Hank was wrong. I was right!*

CHAPTER TWENTY-SIX

Hank left the kitchen heading towards the hallway to see who had buzzed the outside gate.

Johnny strained to listen to what was going on and heard Hank exclaim, "Oh shit."

Johnny scanned the kitchen to see what he could use as a weapon. All he spied was a couple of steak knives. He palmed one as he heard Hank press the buzzer, the one that Johnny assumed would open the gate.

From his position in the kitchen, he could hear Hank open the front door and give someone a cheery greeting. *Hmm, if it was a cartel death squad he would not sound like that,* Johnny thought. Still, he remained tense and ready for anything.

Now he heard Hank speaking in Spanish and some giggling. *Females?*

Joe and Johnny stared in awe as they were greeted to three females in very tight, very short dresses and high heels made up to the nines.

"Well look who Momo sent over to keep us company," declared Hank with a huge smile on his face.

At first glance the oldest woman appeared to be mid-forties and the younger two appeared to be mid-twenties. Joe and Hank were actually blushing.

Hank rushed to the fridge and produced beers for the newcomers and introduced Joe and Johnny to the ladies.

The oldest one was Sofia and the younger two were Maria and Isabel, apparently.

Johnny assumed they were hookers on the cartel's payroll sent to service clients. Regardless of the gesture he was adamant to stay on high alert. He had heard of brothers traveling to Asia hiring sex workers only to wake up the next day to find they had been robbed. He was too smart to fall for that.

After a couple more beers a bottle of tequila magically appeared and everyone started doing shots. Johnny went to piss and on his return, he found Hank and Joe standing outside the kitchen in a heated discussion.

"Problems?" he asked his club brothers.

Hank looked at Johnny. "No, no problems. Joe wants Sofia and wants me to take Isabel, that's all."

"Oh geez." Johnny laughed. "I'll leave you two to sort that out."

Johnny returned and the three ladies toasted him with more tequila shots. He hated to admit it, but he was starting to feel very drunk. Then he had a brain wave. He still had the sample pack of coke that Momo had gifted him. At the next available opportunity, he would hit the bathroom and do a couple of bumps to straighten himself out.

Clearly Joe and Hank had resolved their shared dilemma. Both men returned to the kitchen, paired off with their respective ladies and made their excuses, taking their "dates" back to their separate rooms.

Joe took the forty-five-year-old Sofia and Hank went off with the mid-twenty-something Isabel. Johnny mentally chuckled at the thought of the able bodied twenty-five-year-old and Hank, Christ, she would probably give the old geezer a heart attack!

The remaining Maria looked shyly at Johnny now that they were alone. Truth be told he had no interest in banging a woman who could be his daughter and didn't trust her enough to just got to sleep.

He turned to her and said, "You like to party?"

She looked at him slightly confused. The expression on her face was like, "*Isn't that what we are already doing? Having a party?*"

"Ah, party," he repeated, this time grabbing his nostrils and making an exaggerated pulling gesture on them.

"Ohh party! Sure, sure," she replied with a smile.

Johnny didn't want to take her back to his room, in case she got the wrong idea about him. Then he remembered the rooftop patio.

"Come with me," he said, grabbing her by the hand and leading her to the stairs to the roof.

The weather on the roof top was actually perfect. It had cooled down significantly since the day's ride but was not in any way chilly. Somewhere in the distance he could hear the waves crashing along the Malecon.

Turned out Maria was very cool and also somewhat decent in English. He had racked out enough lines to last them all night and before he knew it the sun was starting to rise along the Eastern Horizon.

Even in the early hours Johnny could feel it starting to warm up. It was going to be another hot day. He was also keen to see what state Joe and Hank were in.

"Shall we head back downstairs?" he suggested to Maria.

"Sure, let's go," she replied. Apparently, she was just as keen to see where her friends (colleagues?) were as well.

They returned to the kitchen to find a very disheveled Joe and an immaculate Sofia.

"Good night?" asked Johnny with a cheeky look on his face.

"Uh, yeah," Joe replied sheepishly. "I'll tell ya in a few."

"Where's the old man? Is he still alive?" asked Johnny.

"I'll go look," offered Sofia, who exited the kitchen.

Joe eyed up Johnny. "All good brother?"

"Yeah! Never been better," Johnny replied. He had long passed that nervy, twitchy stage of coke use and was currently on an even keel. He was sure as the day went on he would be feeling it though.

Sofia returned to the kitchen.

"The old man is sleeping, everything is fine."

No sooner had she finished explaining this, Isabel turned up with a smile on her face.

"We will leave now. I hope you both had fun," Sofia explained.

"Ah, well um okay, nice to meet you all," Joe said rather sheepishly and awkwardly. Johnny gave a half assed wave to Maria. He watched as Joe walked them out the front door and to the front gate, making small talk.

When he returned, he turned to Johnny.

"What do ya think?" he asked Johnny.

"About what?" Johnny replied, meaning Joe could be asking his opinion on a hundred different topics.

"You think the old man is sleeping or dead?" Joe asked all seriously.

"Ahh I'm sure he's just sleeping." Johnny dismissed it as nothing to be worried about. "Shall we go grab breakfast and come back from him?"

"Yeah, sounds good, I could do with some food. I have the gate codes from Hank so we should be good to get back in."

"Okay, let's go and grab breakfast," Johnny suggested.

CHAPTER TWENTY-SEVEN

It was only after they found a breakfast place a couple of blocks away on the main road that they realized they probably should have woken Hank up. None of the staff at the breakfast place they found open could speak any English and of course Joe and Johnny knew about four words of Spanish between them. They had to settle for pointing at images and nodding their heads to order in the end.

Over breakfast burritos and coffee, Joe asked Johnny, "So, how was your chick?"

Johnny wasn't in the mood as he was more concerned about their impending delivery of product and the return trip to Arizona. "What? Oh yeah Maria, yeah cool chick."

"Nice, nice," Joe replied. "Mine was incredible. She did things to my cock I didn't even know were possible."

"Bro, c'mon, I'm trying to eat my breakfast. I don't wanna hear about your cock you dirty bastard," Johnny snapped at him.

"Sorry bro, had to share." Joe laughed.

All Johnny could do was shake his head in disgust. There was a time and place for this. It was called Friday night at the bar with a few beers, not breakfast burritos and coffee.

The duo headed back. Joe spied a small hole-in-the-wall bike shop on the road back to their place.

Since the shop wasn't open yet he peered through the glass to get a better look.

"He,y check this place. They got a couple of vintage Harleys in there," Joe commented.

"That's cool," said Johnny.

"I didn't think we would find 'em here," Joe replied. "They got a bunch of those bikes Hank rides, Ithakas or whatever he calls them. I see a Honda too."

"Yeah, I heard Honda has a factory down here or something," Johnny added. "C'mon, let's go back and see if Hank is up yet."

Upon returning to their villa, they found a shirtless Hank stumbling around the kitchen.

"Ah he lives!" Joe laughed. "We thought you might have died with a smile on your face last night."

Hank grumbled, "Ugh, I just need some juice and to go back to bed for an hour more. You boys got breakfast, I assume?"

"Yeah, we figured it out without ya buddy," Johnny teased.

'That's a first," quipped Hank. "Let me guess. Point at pics on the menu and shout loudly in English?"

"Yeah, something like that," Johnny replied.

Hank grabbed some juice and made his way out of the kitchen. Joe turned to Johnny and said, "Hey, thats not a bad idea. I am gonna head back to bed and grab some more shut eye. You should too."

"Yeah, think I will," Johnny replied. After Joe left the kitchen, he contemplated going back to bed but was worried he might miss the delivery guys.

He went back to his room and grabbed his baggy and took a couple of small bumps just to stay up and wait for the delivery.

CHAPTER TWENTY-EIGHT

Despite doing coke all night, Johnny actually drifted off there for a while. He was not sure if it was fifteen minutes or an hour later but he was surprised when he came to. He had done enough coke with Maria to keep an entire squadron of men awake overnight. Perhaps it was like rebooting a computer to get it working again. Either way, it surprised him, and he actually felt okay.

He heard noise back down in the kitchen again, so he pulled his engineer boots back on and went down the stairs to investigate.

There he found Hank stuffing himself with a bag of potato chips and sipping on coffee.

"Hey," Hank said between mouthfuls.

"How you doing?" asked Johnny.

"Drank way too much last night, but no complaints, all good. You?" Hank replied.

"Yep, same," said Johnny. "Any news from Momo's people?"

"Yeah, they just texted. Be arriving here around 1 p.m.," Hank explained.

"Okay, great," Johnny replied. "And then we head home yeah?"

"That's the plan!" Hank smiled. "I'll ride with you guys all the way up to Imuris and then I'll be heading home"

"Wait, where's Imuris?" asked Johnny.

"Just before Nogales," Hank explained. "That's my road home to Juarez and you have a way over the border near Nogales, right?"

"Oh okay," Johnny replied. "Yeah, I do."

Hank grabbed his cup of coffee. "I'm going to go and watch TV until they get here, you coming?"

Johnny thought for a moment. "Nah, I'm gonna go back to my room and rest, see ya in a few old man."

Johnny left the kitchen and headed back upstairs.

CHAPTER TWENTY-NINE

Despite all the coke he had done, Johnny felt himself fighting exhaustion and sleep and soon he had passed back out on his bed fully clothed. Not sure how long he was out for, he was awakened by a long and drawn-out buzz from the front door. *That's got to be them,* he thought.

Johnny pulled his boots on and went and knocked on Joe's door. "Hey, wake up sleeping beauty, the delivery man is here."

"Huh? Whaaa?" Joe replied, clearly woken up mid-sleep.

"Pull some clothes on and get downstairs bro," Johnny replied before leaving Joe's door and heading down to help Hank with the hand over.

As he was descending the stairs he could see Hank holding the front door open as two men bought in a bunch of grocery carry bags. Johnny eyed the guys up. Neither looked particularly threatening or dangerous; in fact, they were of slight build and just wearing regular clothes you would see on any Saturday afternoon downtown shopper. *Makes sense,* he guessed. Be invisible by blending in.

Hank turned back and nodded at Johnny as he came down the stairs. The delivery guys left the packages on the kitchen countertop and said something to Hank in Spanish. Hank replied, "Gracias mis amigos, les gustaria una cerveza helada?"

Johnny heard, "Thanks friends and cerverzas," out of the entire conversation.

The two guys looked a little worried, shook their heads and pointed at their car like they needed to leave right away.

Hank shrugged and walked them out to their car. After seeing them off he returned to the house closing the front door behind him.

"What was that about?" asked Johnny.

"Ahh I just asked them if they wanted a beer. Figured it was the polite thing to do, ya know?" Hank explained.

"Yeah, I get it. I guess they're under strict orders not to fraternize with the clients, or they are on a tight schedule," suggested Johnny.

"Yeah, one or the other, or a bit of both." Hank shrugged. "Either way, no biggie."

"Yep," said Johnny. "So this is it?" he asked, looking over the shopping bags stacked up on the counter top.

"Yeah, the answer to all your problems." Hank smiled. "Hey, where's Joe?"

"He should be down in a sec. He was out cold when I went past his room," Johnny explained.

Johnny entered the kitchen and examined the kilos. "Hey, you got any packing tape or scotch tape?" he asked Hank.

Hank pulled open a bunch of kitchen cabinets, finally finding a roll of packing tape. Johnny grabbed a sharp knife out of the utensils' drawer and two random kilos of cocaine. He made a small slit into the first package and very carefully extracted a bump of coke on the edge of the knife. He held one nostril closed and snorted. *Oof!* Right away, the powerful powder ripped through his brain. *Oh shit this stuff is gooood,* he thought as his brain started firing on all cylinders. He repeated the process on the second package but used his other nostril this time.

He turned to Hank with a silly grin on his face. "Yep, this is the real deal."

"I told ya." Hank nodded.

"Yeah, I just didn't want us getting stiffed, that's all," Johnny explained.

"Yeah, I get it," Hank replied. "These guys don't mess around."

"I see that now," Johnny replied, grabbing the packing tape and taping up the slits he had made in the two packages.

Joe finally came downstairs and entered the room. "Oh shit it's here!" he exclaimed.

"Yeah, I just grabbed two kilos at random and tested them, 100% pure shit man," Johnny said.

"Oh, you think we should test all of them?" Joe asked.

"Nah, I reckon we are good. Hank says these guys don't fuck about," Johnny replied.

"So what's our plan then?" asked Joe.

"I figure we finish off here, grab our gear, load the bikes and start the journey home," Hank said.

"That works for me," Joe said. "How long will it take us to get back to Arizona from here?"

"Hmm, probably two days," Hank replied. "Normal tourists would take the 15 Highway north but considering what we're carrying, we are going to take some back roads, if ya get me."

"Yeah, good call," Johnny replied. "I don't fancy getting stopped by your federales with these babies," he said, slapping the top of one of the kilos.

"No sir, we do not want that." Hank laughed. "Let's take ten minutes to pack your bags and then we can load the bikes, alright?"

Johnny looked at the clock, 1:45 p.m.. They should be out the door and moving by 2 p.m. with any luck.

Five minutes later everyone was packed and ready to go. Despite there being a nice privacy wall between them and the street they decided it would be best to bring Johnny and Joe's bikes as close as possible to the front door of the villa for the load out. Joe's hard-shell panniers were slightly larger than Johnny's so he managed to put all twenty kilos into his without issue. Johnny could only manage eighteen in his saddle bags, so he decided to toss out some used T-shirts and boxers to fit the final two keys into his backpack.

Heck, with all the money he stood to make selling the dope state side he could buy gold plated T-shirts.

The trio gave their scoots a quick dummy check to make sure nothing had shaken loose from their last ride and fired up their bikes for the long ride home. Soon they were following old man Hank back out on to the city streets navigating their way through the afternoon traffic out of town.

CHAPTER THIRTY

After passing through a nice leafy suburban area, they soon found themselves entering an industrial neighborhood. Johnny figured Hank was more than likely taking them the path less travelled to avoid running into local cops. Fine by him. He had no idea what the penalty would be for getting caught with this much blow. Who knows? Maybe nothing? Maybe 400 years hard labor in the worst prison in all of Mexico. (He had heard horror stories of these prisons where they just throw you in there and you have to fend for yourself. Guards don't go in; their sole job is just to make sure you never get out. Terrifying.)

They passed a lot of old warehouses, some seemingly desolate and others barely hanging on. As they rounded the next corner, to Johnny's horror he saw that there were two masked men standing up in the flat bed of a Ford pick-up truck. Both were wearing camo gear, and one was leaning on a mounted fifty caliber.

Oh fuck, that stupid old man has led us right into a bunch of federales! Thought Johnny.

To his surprise, the one not resting on the high-powered rifle gave them a small wave as they passed by.

Okay phew, false alarm, thought Johnny. *Panicking over nothing.*

Out of his peripheral vision he saw the man who waved at him shout something to a person, or persons, unseen deep in the warehouse they were parked in front of. *Not hanging around to see what happens next,* Johnny thought to himself.

They were just taking a right turn at the end of the block when Johnny sensed movement. He cranked his neck back to see what was going on and spotted two men on bikes and a beat up car can flying out of the warehouse heading their way. *Oh shit, we are going to have company very, very soon,* Johnny figured.

He twisted his throttle and pulled in front of Hank, madly gesticulating that they had to go faster or take evasive action. Johnny figured Hank might have got the hint as he took a quick left turn down the nearest alley before their pursuers could see them. *Smart thinking, old man,* thought Johnny, following just feet behind the old geezer. He could feel Joe's bike just feet behind his as well.

They took a quick left after exiting the alley way. What was Hank thinking? Maybe circle back behind them? Sure enough, they got to the end of this road and took a hard left again bringing them back to the block they were on originally before taking the alley way detour.

No sign of their pursuers, perhaps Hank had lost them after all. They hightailed it to the end of the street. Hank was waving that they had to turn right at the end of the block. Johnny risked looking back over his shoulder to see if they had been followed and spotted one of the motorcyclists now appearing at the top of the block. He must have followed them out of the alley and back the way they had ridden. But where was the other rider and the car?

They turned right and Hank slammed on his brakes. Johnny had to struggle to not low side his Harley to avoid running Hank down. He could hear Joe screeching to a halt behind him too. He looked up to see the beat-up old car and two armed gun men blocking the road smiling at them.

In his rear view mirror, he could see the second biker rapidly approaching. He must have turned right out of the alley where the first biker had gone left. Smart, that's what Johnny would have done if he was giving chase too.

Hank put his quick stand down and turning to Johnny and Joe, hissing, "Let me handle this!"

Crazy old bastard was about to get himself shot up, thought Johnny as Hank approached the men speaking in Spanish.

The men smiled back, pointing at Joe and Johnny speaking in rapid fire Spanish.

Hank replied. Johnny felt helpless, no clue whatsoever on what was being said. For all he knew Hank was selling them out to save his own skin.

The men spoke again to Hank. He tried to read their body language. They didn't seem hostile or aggressive, but then again that was a common technique many street fighters used. Instead of tensed up, red faced and shouting at you, they approach with a relaxed body posture and a friendly smile. Just to give you a false sense of security before popping ya. He had his pistol smuggled in his tool roll from Phoenix but there was no way he could access it in time to save their skins.

The two bikers had now pulled up behind them but gave themselves some distance between Joe and Johnny's bikes and theirs. Johnny hazarded a glance at them, and they were smiling too. Was this all some sick game?

One of the two men who had travelled in the car said something to Hank and gestured for him to get closer to their car. *Oh shit,* thought Johnny, *This is bad....*

The man popped the trunk and rummaged around for a moment before pulling out a crumpled book or magazine and started waving it in front of Hank's face, pointing at something on the page. From his position he couldn't see what it was but figured now might be the time to open his tool roll which was strapped to his handlebars. This was going to turn bad, fast.

CHAPTER THIRTY-ONE

Johnny started fiddling with his tool roll, making out he was tightening one of the straps or just messing with it. He hoped the men behind him were not watching him closely. He would not survive an out and out shoot out with these guys, but in close quarters it might even the playing field enough for him and Joe to make their escape.

He managed to undo the first buckle when Hank suddenly turned and started walking back towards the bikes. He had his hands raised slightly, not all the way up in a "hands up don't shoot position" but more of a peacekeeper type position.

"What the hell is going on?" asked Joe.

"Look, here's the deal," explained Hank. "These guys are fans of the Steel Reapers, that one guy even has a support calendar from 2008 in the trunk of his car."

"What? They recognized us from that?" asked Johnny incredulously.

"Yeah, apparently they are big fans of the Steel Reapers MC." Hank shrugged.

"Okay soooo... what does that mean for us?" asked Joe.

"Oh," laughed Hank, "they just want a selfie or two with you guys and we are good to go."

"That's it?" asked Joe. "Well, why didn't you say so? Let's do it and get on our way."

Johnny didn't really feel like playing anyone's role model, but he was relived that's all they wanted from them. "Sure, fine."

Hank turned and spoke to the guys by the car again. They came forwards, leaving their guns on the hood of their car. They gestured to their friends behind the trio to come forwards too. The driver handed Hank his cell phone to act as photographer.

The six men all huddled together, arms on each other's shoulders.

"Bien, todos aprietense, sonrian, sonrian," Hank instructed.

Johnny assumed it was Spanish for, "Everyone say cheese." Too bad he had a personal rule never to smile in photographs.

After taking a couple of pics, Hank handed the cell phone back to the leader of the group.

He said a few more things in Spanish that Johnny couldn't figure out, but he assumed were goodbyes.

"We all good now?" asked Johnny.

"Yeah, yeah, just saying our goodbyes," Hank explained.

Joe and Johnny started pulling on their helmets and waved at the cartel guys to say goodbye.

"C'mon old man, we are burning daylight," Joe shouted.

"Yeah, yeah, give me a sec," Hank replied, saying some final words to the two men by the car.

Hank shook hands with both men and made a gesture to get back on his bike. The two cartel guys were all smiles as they waved goodbye and headed back towards the warehouse they had come from.

As the car pulled out, the two riders fired up their bikes and followed the car back towards their place.

Finally, it was time to go again, and Joe and Johnny followed Hank as he navigated the Mazatlan streets towards the highway north.

They found the on ramp and started to pick up speed with the afternoon traffic heading north. Despite having enjoyed himself the last few days, great food, picturesque scenery and amazing small towns Johnny was glad to be making a bee line for home, especially with their cargo they were carrying on their bikes.

CHAPTER THIRTY-TWO

No sooner had that gotten to top speed than Hank started making the signal for them to pull off at the next exit. *WTF? This guy who busted my balls for the last few days for multiple bathroom breaks now needs a bathroom break?* thought Johnny. *We've only been riding for ten minutes!*

They took the exit ramp with Joe and Johnny trailing behind Hank.

They pulled into a small driveway, a short distance past the exit ramp.

Joe put down his kick stand, pulled off his helmet and headed over to Hank.

"Everything alright old man?" he asked.

"Yeah, all good here, we have to take surface roads from here on out," Hank explained. "Too many toll booths and federales on the highway north."

"Ah okay, good thinking, I like it," Johnny replied. "I was gonna say, it's unlike you to need a bathroom break so soon after leaving Mazatlan."

"Nah, nah not me, that's you and Joe's domain." Hank laughed.

"Okay so we all set?" asked Hank. "Just follow me, alright?"

They continued down the side road that ran perpendicular to the highway for about three miles–again a lot of twists and turns that took extreme concentration from Johnny's coke addled brain to not low side and crash. Roll off the throttle, counter steer, roll back on the throttle, roll off again, counter steer to the other side and repeat.

Hank waved his left hand off to the left, the signal that they would be turning soon. Reducing speed, Johnny looked for the road they were aiming for. It wasn't until the last moment did he spy a car's wide gap between two fences. *That's where we're headed?* The road wasn't paved but it was hard packed dirt, telling him that at one point or another a lot of vehicular traffic had been down this way. Their bikes would have no problems riding this dirt as long as it didn't loosen up. They were now running parallel to the highway again, once more heading north towards home.

Johnny was surprised they were making good time on this dirt road. Not having to battle with freight trucks and vacationing families in soccer mom wagons made the ride much more enjoyable.

About two miles into heading north, Johnny felt his rear tire locking up; something was wrong, very wrong. He fought with his Harley to bring it to a stop without high siding him and managed to get to the side of the road. There was scrub and twenty-five feet past that was a cliff side drop off. He was relieved he hadn't gone over the edge there and had come to a controlled stop. But what the hell was wrong with his scoot?

Joe pulled up behind him and Hank, and, realizing something was wrong, swung back in a U-turn to get back to them.

Shutting down his Mexican made bike, Hank shouted, "What happened?"

"Rear wheel locked up!" Johnny shouted back.

Joe dashed over. "Dude your chain broke! Nearly blinded me."

'What?" gasped Johnny.

He looked down, and his chain was gone. Upon a closer examination he could see a piece of chain had wedged between his rear tire and the back sprocket. *FUCK*!

"Of all the places to break down," cursed Johnny. "FUCK!!!"

Joe had grabbed a couple of screwdrivers from his tool roll and knelt down by Johnny's scoot.

"Hey, it could have been worse, way worse," Hank said.

"How do you figure?" asked Johnny.

"Well, if we had been on that highway and your rear wheel had locked up you could have been run over by an eighteen-wheeler," Hank explained. "Think of that."

"Yeah, true." Johnny sighed.

"Hey, I got the piece of chain out," Joe proudly announced. Joe grabbed the remaining pieces of bike chain and held them up.

"Anyone got a chain tool?" he asked.

"Yeah, I got one in my tool roll," Johnny said. "But ain't gonna be long enough. I've lost too much."

Joe and Hank thought for a moment. Joe looked at his watch.

"Hey, what about that cycle shop I saw back in town?" Joe asked.

"There's a motorcycle shop in Mazatlan?" asked Hank.

"Yeah, like a block from the villa we were staying in," explained Joe. "It's just after four. I could ride back, grab a replacement chain and be back here for like 5:30, latest 6 p.m."

"Hmm, definitely do-able," Hank said. "You need the address of the villa for your GPS?"

"Yeah, I think if I can get back there, I can find the shop, it's literally a block away," Joe replied.

Hank gave him the street address for Momo's villa. Joe got ready to leave.

"Whoa whoa, stop!" shouted Johnny.

"What's wrong bro?" asked Joe.

"You are carrying twenty keys of primo coke brother," Johnny replied. "You need to stash it here just in case you're stopped, right?"

"Fuck, yeah, good thinking," Joe said.

"Actually, thinking about it," Hank added, "we should stash all the coke, not just Joe's."

"Oh yeah? Why would you think that?" asked Johnny, eying Hank suspiciously.

"Joe leaves, let's say the local cops drive by. They stop to see if we need help. They search your saddle bags... boom we're busted!"

"He's right you know," Joe replied. "Look over here. Down the path." Joe pointed to some bushes about fifty feet away from them. "We can bury it there and collect it once your bike is fixed."

Johnny looked to see where Joe was pointing. *That could work. That could actually work.*

Johnny followed the path that ran parallel to the dirt road. The ground near the second bush was soft enough he could loosen it with his boot. He got on his knees and started digging like a dog.

"Yeah, this could work," Johnny announced. "It's close enough for us to keep an eye out but not close enough for the cops to search, I reckon."

"Okay cool. That settles it," Hank said. "Joe, let's get you offloaded so you can get back to the bike store in time."

The trio made a chain gang, Joe removing the kilos from his panniers and passing them to Hank who in turn handed them to Johnny. Johnny carried them to the bush and returned. Within minutes they had emptied Joe's bike of all the cocaine.

"Alright, you guys cool if I leave now or do you need help with Johnny's stash?" asked Joe.

"Nah, nah. You go. Me and the old man can move mine. Just get to the shop and come straight back," Johnny urged his friend.

"Okay then, I'm out of here. See you boys in an hour, well, ninety minutes tops," Joe said. He kicked his bike in gear and tore out, heading south at top speed.

It took Johnny and Hank about twenty minutes to move his keys, dig the hole and bury their packages. Hank even went as far as brushing the pathway down to remove their trail of boot prints back and forth, so if some eagle-eyed investigator did happen along them they would not get curious and investigate the fresh dirt under the brush.

Hank sat down by their bikes. "Phew, I'm worn out now, ya want a shot?" he asked, waving his hip flask in the air.

"Whiskey?" asked Johnny.

"Nah, Tequila. When in Rome son, when in Rome," Hank replied.

"Okay that works," Johnny said, grabbing the hip flask from Hank and taking a long swig.

"Ahh, thanks," Johnny said, passing it back to the aging biker.

Hank and Johnny shot the shit about the old days of the club, causing havoc all the way from Tucson to Phoenix and all points north.

"They were great days," Hank reminisced. "Even the times when we were in fear of our lives."

"Yeah, some of those club wars, I thought we were both goners ya know." Johnny laughed. "Fuck, how are we still alive?"

Hank looked at his watch; it was after 5 p.m.

"You know, we should probably think about camping here for the night," he suggested.

"Sleep here?" Johnny snapped, quickly taken back. "You don't have hotels set up for us?"

"Nah, not on this leg brother," Hank explained. "I figured we could pull over one night and sleep by the side of the road like we used to in the '80s for one night and the next night you would be back over the border."

"Well shit, I don't have a tent or anything," Johnny explained.

"I got a pup tent but it only sleeps one," Hank replied. "I've got some space blankets though. You're welcome to have one of those."

"Space blankets? What are they?" he asked.

"They're super lightweight blankets treated with an aluminum coating that traps your body heat in 'em," Hank explained.

"Fuck, why can't we just keep riding?" asked Johnny.

"The way I figure it, by the time Joe returns he's gonna be tired and it will be too dark to work on your bike until dawn. We camp out, fix your bike in the morning then hit the road right after first light," said Hank.

"What about food?" asked Johnny. "I have nothing."

Hank thought for a moment. "I've got some protein bars in my pack. That will keep us going until morning bro."

Johnny didn't like it, but it was starting to make sense. It would probably be dark by the time Joe got back.

Hank went to his saddle bags and started fishing out his camping gear. He pulled out a small tent and started looking for a place to set up.

"We might want to think about pushing our bikes back off the side of the road," he suggested. "We don't want to be sleeping and attract the wrong type of attention."

Johnny thought for a moment. "Yeah, good call. How about over there?" asked Johnny, pointing to a small clearing in the opposite direction from where their stash was buried.

"Yeah, that could work," Hank replied.

The pair pushed their bikes out of sight from the main road and set up in the middle of the clearing Johnny had suggested. Hank set up his pup tent to the right of the bikes. He fished around in his saddle bags some more, eventually finding those space blankets he had been telling Johnny about.

"Hey, I have a bunch of these. Until Joe gets back you could use one as a ground sheet and the other to cover yourself." He handed the lightweight space blankets to Johnny.

Johnny examined them; they didn't look like much. "Okay, thanks. I was planning on using my jacket as a blanket but if you think this is superior then I'll use it."

"They work, trust me," Hank replied.

It was now 6:45 p.m. and Joe should have been back by now.

"Hey, Joe should have been back by now," Johnny explained. "I think I am going to call him."

"Yeah, good thinking," Hank replied. "Let me know if he's stuck or lost somewhere will ya?"

"Yeah, will do," Johnny responded.

He hit Joe's number in his phone and waited as it connected.

He could hear a ringing. Hank heard it too. "What the fuck?" Hank asked.

They walked back to where they had originally pulled over. Sure enough, there was Joe's cell phone in the dirt. He must have dropped it unloading his packages.

"Fuck," Johnny shouted. "He's on his own now."

"Look Ace, don't sweat it. If he's not back by morning, I'll ride out and find him. Best we can do for now is sit tight."

"Yeah, you're right." Johnny shrugged. "I can't believe this fucker dropped his cell phone."

"Well, it's Joe. That's totally something he would do," Hank reasoned.

"Yeah, true." Johnny sighed. He loved Joe like a little brother, but he was never the sharpest knife in the drawer.

"What do you think happened to him?" asked Johnny.

"Well, I reckon he got there in no time and figured he would have time to hit the bar and have a quick beer," reasoned Hank. "That's my best guess."

"Or maybe he met some Big Booty Latina?" joked Johnny.

"Yeah, that too. He will probably be along soon enough," Hank replied.

"You don't think he's meeting those cartel guys and striking a deal on his own, do ya?" asked Johnny.

"What? No! Of course not. Geez." Hank shook his head. "Why would you even think like that?"

"Just running through possibilities in my head," Johnny explained.

"Well don't. Nothing good can come from that form of thinking, Ace," Hank replied.

"You think we should build a fire or something?" asked Johnny.

Just as Hank was weighing up the pros and cons of building a fire, a truck came along. It had to be the first vehicle using this road since they broke down. Both Johnny and Hank froze, not daring to make a sound.

From his vantage point off the road, as far as Johnny could see, it looked like two farmers heading home. Then again in this part of the world if they were farmers, what were they farming? Poppies? Weed?

"Maybe it's best we don't set a fire," said Johnny after the truck had passed them.

"Yeah, I'm thinking that might be smart," Hank replied "We could attract cartel guys or worse, the federales"

"Yeah, fuck that," Johnny replied. "Hey, I gotta go and take a piss, be right back."

"I'll be here." Hank laughed. "Not like I got anywhere else to go."

Johnny went to piss. He tapped his back pocket and realized he still had his personal stash of cocaine on him. *Fuck it, probably won't hurt to stay alert,* he reasoned and took a couple of bumps while still taking a piss. It was dusk now, but he still wiped his nose carefully to make sure no coke residue remained around his nostrils.

All he needed was some over eager cop with a flashlight in his face to spot the evidence and it wouldn't end well.

When he returned, he saw Hank sitting cross-legged in the dirt between his tent and where Johnny had laid out the space blankets. As Johnny got closer, he could see two protein bars lying on the blankets.

"That's for you," Hank explained. "I've got one more for Joe too. He's gonna be hungry when he returns, I reckon."

"Thanks old man, I would be screwed without ya," Johnny replied. "Got any more of that tequila?"

"Here ya go," Hank said, tossing his hip flask at Johnny. "Save me a lil, would ya?"

"Sure," Johnny replied, taking a decent swig. The booze put him in a good spot. His heart was racing, his brain was racing and the tequila sort of leveled him out. Talk about making the best of a shit situation.

CHAPTER THIRTY-THREE

It was after 9 p.m. now. Johnny had mentally given up on Joe showing up any time tonight now. *Whatever happens next, we will have to figure it out in the morning*, he had decided. Just have to roll with the punches at this point. There was really nothing more he could do.

Somewhere in Hank's saddle bags he had found another bottle of Tequila. Johnny guessed when your bike wasn't loaded down with kilos of cocaine, you do actually have room to carry other essential items.

Hank had a nice buzz going now. Johnny was still doing that high wire balancing act of boozing and snorting coke. He did feel like he was on an "even keel" mentally and physically but the reality was he was half toasted and half blasted. *Well, what else could you do when you were broken down somewhere in the middle of Mexico lord knows how far from civilization?* Just gotta enjoy yourself and go with the flow.

There was no artificial light anywhere to be seen in any direction from their current position. No houses, no farms, no streetlights, no nothing. There was, however, a vast sky full of stars, something Johnny hadn't seen since his childhood growing up in Tucson. He looked up at awe at the clusters of stars that covered the entire night sky. He wondered if someone was up there looking down and watching them in their current predicament waiting to see what they did next. Probably. Who knows?

Around 10 p.m., Hank announced he was going to try and sleep.

"We should think about wrapping it up Ace," Hank explained. "Joe will probably be back at first light and we wanna be well rested. Make the repairs that we need and get on our way before we lose any more time."

"Yeah, I get ya," Johnny replied. "See ya in the morning brother."

Hank crawled into his pup tent, leaving Johnny with his makeshift bed of two space blankets, his jacket and his boots bunched up as a makeshift pillow. He had done multiple road trips all through the '80s camping like this (well, with proper blankets or a sleeping bag) but it was a thousand times easier to do it when you were young, dumb and in your twenties compared to your early sixties. He longed for his comfy bed and some clean sheets. He lay there and tried to clear his mind, which was swimming in a sea of Tequila and white powder. With his eyes scrunched tight he tried to clear his mind of all thoughts, but it was next to impossible. *Weren't there deadly scorpions in Mexico? What about snakes?*

Fuck! These stupid space blankets were not going to do it for him. At least with a sleeping bag a snake or scorpion had only one spot to crawl into your bed (the open end), but with a flimsy space blanket they could get in anywhere they chose. Johnny made up his mind; he would do a bump from his personal stash of coke and stay up all night. It would be the only way he could ensure that he wouldn't get bitten in the middle of the night. He got up out of his makeshift bed and retrieved his pistol from his tool roll too. Any deadly rattlers that come this way were going to get a lead ventilation, he decided.

Returning to his bed he kept his pistol by his right side. He slipped the safety off, figuring he needed to be ready for any snakes that came slithering his way. While sitting up he took a couple of bumps from his never-ending coke stash and lay back down. For some silly reason he began grinning like an idiot at the thought of the predicament he was in. Lying on a flimsy silvery blanket in the dirt at the age of sixty-two with his well-worn and oily engineer boots as a pillow and his trusted leather jacket as an extra blanket. Lost somewhere in the back roads of Sinaloa with a crazy old man he hadn't seen in twenty years and his best friend unaccounted for. What were his poor life choices that led him here? Oh well, didn't matter now; the main thing was to get his scoot fixed, retrieve their hidden stash and head north. If all went well, they would be back in Phoenix in forty-eight hours. Not bad, not bad at all. Sell the product, pay off the bank and buy back his beloved chopper. That was all that mattered now.

He got up and walked to the edge of the cliff side, grateful that the stars were out tonight to illuminate his path and took a piss over the edge of the cliff. If it had been a cloudy night, he could have easily walked right off the edge of the ravine if he didn't have a flashlight. He shuddered at the thought.

It had to be past 11 p.m. by now and he returned to his makeshift dirt bed to give one more attempt to try and get a little shut eye. He recalled reading an article about successful men once, where many of them said even a fifteen-minute power nap can do wonders for the brain. Almost like a computer reboot. If he could even get just fifteen minutes, he would see that as an accomplishment.

He lay on his back with his head resting on his old boots. Heck they were actually kinda comfortable as a pillow. Well at least for one night. He stared up at the millions of stars. Was the trying to spot a UFO or a shooting star? He wasn't sure, just looking and thinking. Somehow despite all the booze and drugs he put into his system today, he actually fell asleep.

Johnny wasn't sure how long he was out for, but it was still dark and someone was walking around. Wait, someone was walking around near where they had buried their stash. He looked over at Hank's tent. It looked closed. Maybe a cop or a homeless person. Fuck, he had better investigate. Ever so carefully, he stayed low and pulled on his boots, fumbling for his pistol in the dark, grateful it was racked and ready to rock 'n roll. He got to his feet and crept over to where they had buried his stash to investigate.

CHAPTER THIRTY-FOUR

In the darkness he could see a shape walking around the tree they had buried their stash at. *How the fuck did they know where to look? Had Joe tipped this person off?* he wondered.

Johnny crept nearer and nearer, if he was going to get into a shoot-out he wanted to be sure he got the drop on the thief first. In the twilight he was planning on taking no chances on taking this rat out. He was now no more than ten feet away from the scumbag.

He raised his pistol and sighted the shape.

"Get on your fuckin' knees now scumbag!" Johnny shouted. "I will shoot you dead. I am not playing around!"

"Whoa, whoa, whoa!" the voice in the dark shouted back.

"On your knees fucker." Johnny was amped up. No way was he letting some scumbag steal his stash after all of this.

"Ace, calm down you idiot, it's me!" the voice said.

"Hank?" Johnny asked, not sure if his ears were deceiving him.

"Yes, it's me! It's Hank! You know, the old man!" Hank shouted. "Put the damn gun down."

"Fuck," Johnny swore. "What are you doing at my stash?"

"I heard someone or something out here, so I got up to investigate," Hank explained.

"I didn't hear anything but you," Johnny said, still holding his pistol towards Hank.

"You were dead to the world Ace," Hank replied.

Johnny strained his eyes to check the dirt near them for footprints.

"I don't see any footprints old man. Just tell me what you were planning to do. Steal our stash and leave us stranded out here?"

"Would you listen to yourself?" Hank said, taking a step closer to Johnny but still holding his hands up. "That makes ZERO sense." Hank paused to get his breath under control. "Why would I introduce you to my guy, let you buy a bunch of product only to rip you off in the middle of nowhere?"

"Because you could take it back to the U.S. and sell it and be set for life down here in Mexico, that's why," Johnny shouted back, still aiming his handgun at the old biker.

"That's preposterous," Hank exclaimed. "Momo could give me as much as I wanted on spec, if I wanted to go down that path. You fool!" Hank took another step close to Johnny.

"Bullshit," Johnny hissed.

"Johnny, listen to me," Hank pleaded. "You're over tired you're not thinking straight. This is madness. I would never even dream of trying to rip you and Joe off."

"Yeah right, Joe is probably in on it with you," Johnny retorted.

"Oh come on Ace, would you listen to yourself. You are just paranoid." Hank sighed, taking another step closer to Johnny.

"Stay back, you thieving fuck!" Johnny warned.

"Put the damn gun down, Ace. We are brothers, remember? We swore an oath to each other once," Hank said, almost sobbing. He took another step closer.

"I warned you," Johnny shouted, putting two bullets into the old man's chest. He went down. Backwards. Into the dirt.

"You shot me! You shot me, you stupid prick. I can't believe you shot me." Hank writhed in pain.

"Shut up, you rat fuck," Johnny replied, putting another bullet into Hank's head. Hank stopped talking, Hank stopped moving.

At that moment, Johnny heard some crashing in the brush past the trees. Was there someone else there?

He ventured further to investigate, being careful not to step off the edge of the cliff to his right. A shape moved in the distance. He strained to see if it was Joe. He took two more slow steps forwards.

Two oxen twenty feet ahead of him moved. *They have random farm animals just wandering around here with no fences? Shit, that must have been what the old man had heard! He was telling the truth after all! Fuck.*

What had he done? Johnny started to panic. No way could he go to prison for murder. Especially not a Mexican prison. He would rather a shoot-out with the feds than face prison. He had to hide the body.

Thinking quickly, he decided the best way to get rid of the old man's body was to toss it down the ravine below. His bike too. He could tell Joe, if Joe even came back, that Hank got fed up waiting and left for home. Yeah, that would work. That would be believable.

He dragged Hank's lifeless corpse to the edge of the ravine. He said a small prayer and rolled the body off the cliff. He could see pools of blood illuminated by the night sky. He kicked dirt with his biker boots to cover the blood and break it up.

Satisfied that he was not leaving any evidence by Hank's body, he went back and checked Hank's bags. He found a small gas can with some gas in it and a quarter of a small bottle of tequila in Hank's tent. He poured that into Hank's hip flask, tossed the empty over the edge of the drop and tossed the now full hip flask back inside the pup tent. He decided to keep the paper map Hank had as well. Pleased that he had scavenged anything of value from Hank's possessions, he pushed the old man's bike to the cliff edge and rolled it over. The chances of anyone finding it any time soon were slim to none, he figured. He heard it clatter down the mountainside before coming to a stop far below.

Without thinking, Johnny grabbed his jacket and helmet and tossed it into Hank's pup tent. He was almost functioning on automatic pilot now. Drunk, high, sleep deprived and he had just murdered his old mentor and club brother, Hank. Strangely, he didn't know what he felt. Remorse? Nah. Worried he would get caught and go to prison? Nah. Bad Karma? Who knows?

He took a couple of good hits from the bottle of tequila and tried to calm himself down. In the morning, he would scour the area to make sure he hadn't left any other incriminating evidence he might have missed in the darkness and toss that over the ravine too.

He lay back down in the tent using the two space blankets to cover himself and his wadded up leather jacket as a pillow. Oddly, he felt way more relaxed in the safety of the flimsy pup tent than he had felt when lying under the stars and soon started drifting off to sleep.

CHAPTER THIRTY-FIVE

Johnny wasn't sure how long he was out for, but it was still dark when he was awoken by the sound of a motorcycle drawing near. He quickly pulled on his jeans and left his boots off. He reached for his pistol before realizing he was inside the old man's tent. He gingerly unzipped it and looked around. The sun was starting to come up over the horizon. What was that? At best guess he figured 5 a.m.? Maybe 5:30 a.m.? The motorcycle was getting closer. It had to be Joe. Where the fuck had he been?

He walked barefoot towards the side of the road. He couldn't see anyone, but he could hear the bike's engine. *What the heck? Was this some kind of cartel stealth attack?*

In the half light, he could finally make out a figure. They were approaching slowly and looking around. Had to be Joe! He slipped his pistol into the waistband of his jeans. *What if it wasn't Joe though?* Johnny was torn.

He decided to crouch low and see what happens next.

Slowly, the rider got closer and closer.

"Johnny, Hank!" the voice whispered.

Shit, it was Joe!

Johnny stood up and waved his arms. The rider swerved and pulled to the right. Joe bought his scoot to a stop just past where Johnny was standing.

He jumped off his bike and ran to Johnny, giving him a big bear hug.

"Holy fuck man. I so am glad to see you," Joe exclaimed.

"Holy fuck bro–what the hell happened?" asked Johnny.

"Oh man, wait till you hear this," Joe said excitably. He went back to his bike and retrieved a package out of his saddle bags.

"Before we get started here, this is yours," Johnny could feel the heavy replacement bike chain in the package.

"Oh shit, thanks," Johnny exclaimed. "What the hell happened man?"

"Oh yeah so, you ready for this?" asked Joe. "I made it in good time back to town and found that lil bike shop with ease."

"Okay, so far, so good," said Johnny.

"I go in there, they have your replacement chain. Perfect, a fair price too. I buy it," Joe continued.

"Okay..." Johnny replied, waiting for Joe to tell him he met a big booty Latina and spent the night buying her drinks.

"I get out of the shop," Joe explained, "and I see someone has smashed my front head light."

"I was wondering about that," said Johnny.

"I was about to go back into the store and see if they had at least a replacement bulb," Joe continued, "when two cops came out of a store front and grabbed me."

"What the fuck?" Johnny exclaimed.

"That's exactly what I said to them!" Joe added. "Yeah, so they cuff me and stuff me into the back of a cruiser they had parked around the corner."

"On what charges?" asked Johnny incredulously.

"Get this," Joe replied, "riding without a headlight!"

"Get the fuck out. Did you explain to them it was fine before you got to the shop?" Johnny asked.

"Hey, I tried, but I don't speak any Spanish," Joe said.

"My bet is they did it just to fuck with you," Johnny guessed.

"Yeah, that was my first thought too," Joe replied. "So they took me downtown and locked me in a cell with a bunch of guys."

"Fuck, how was that?" Johnny asked.

"Well, most seemed more scared of me than anything," Joe explained.

"Hey, not a bad thing," said Johnny.

"Yeah, I agree," Joe replied. "So anyways, I'm locked in there for hours. They finally lock up this local, but he can speak English."

"Alright," said Johnny.

"This dude explained to me they plan to hold me until I can pay a fine," Joe continued.

"Ugh fuck how much?" asked Johnny,

"Five hundred and nine Mexican dollars!" Joe explained.

"Whoa! How much is that in real money?" asked Johnny.

Joe laughed, "Get this, twenty-five!"

"Oh shit," Johnny replied.

"Yeah so, I get my newfound friend to call the guards over, he explains that I want to pay. I pay and they let me out," said Joe.

"Nice! What time was this?" asked Johnny.

"Oh I figure a lil after 1 a.m.," said Joe nonchalantly.

"Dude it's got to be 5 a.m. 6 a.m. by now, please tell me you met a big booty Latina," Johnny added.

"Hell no! Well, I wish," Joe continued. "It took me forever to find where the bike shop was and surprise surprise, my bike was still there."

"Wow, I was expecting you were going to tell me it had been stolen," said Johnny.

"Yeah, I half expected that too," Joe carried on. "So I started making my way back. In the city it wasn't too bad as I could see where I was going with street lights and late night taxis."

"Oh fuck I didn't think about that," said Johnny.

"Yeah, but once out on the open road, I had to wait till a truck came by and let them light the way for me. I couldn't see jack shit," said Joe.

"Good thinking," Johnny added.

"Yeah, I nearly missed the turn off to that side road," Joe continued. "It took me forever to find this dirt road."

"I bet," Johnny replied, thinking if he had been looking for it in the dark, he would have probably ridden right into some farmer's field by mistake.

"Coming up this dirt road it was next to impossible to find where you broke down," Joe added. "I reckon if it was broad daylight I would have found it fairly easy but in the dark without a fire, no chance."

"Dayum son you had quite the night, didn't ya?" said Johnny.

"Yeah, I did" Joe replied. "I never ever want to go through that again."

"Haha, I bet." Johnny laughed.

"To top it all off I lost my cell phone too. I had all my contacts in there. I reckon those local cops stole it," Joe added.

"No, no, you dropped it here, bro," Johnny explained. "I have it. Let me grab it for ya."

Johnny walked back to the tent, reached in, spotted Joe's dropped cell phone, returned and passed it to Joe.

"Thanks," Joe said.

"Anytime brother," Johnny replied.

Joe looked around. "Hey, wait a minute, where's Hank?"

CHAPTER THIRTY-SIX

Hank? Oh Hank." Johnny paused for a moment then explained, "He got pissed off with waiting and went home."

"What? He left you here alone?" Joe asked. "Are you kidding me? That's some bullshit."

"Uh, yeah," Johnny meekly replied.

"I can't believe that fucker," Joe raged. "What if I was in hospital or something? He just left you stuck out here on your own? You could have died out here."

"Uh, yeah," Johnny replied again

"He ain't no brother. Fuck him." Joe was still wounded by the whole affair.

The sun was up now. Johnny was keen to change the subject.

"Shall we try this new chain then eh?" he asked.

It took a moment to get Joe out of his funk. "What? Oh yeah? Let's get it up and running, brother."

It took them about an hour to get Johnny's bike up and running. It would have been a lot easier in a fully equipped shop than by the side of a dirt road somewhere in the middle of Mexico with a handful of tools, but the pair got there in the end. Finally, it was time to pack up and go.

"I don't know about you, but I am fucking starving," Joe declared. "Hopefully there is some diner or at least a food truck somewhere on this road, ya know?"

"Yeah, I hope so," Johnny replied but not really believing they would find anything on such a long-forgotten stretch of road. "Oh, Hank left you a protein bar bro."

"A protein bar? That fuck. That's almost an insult. Would almost be better if he left me nothing," Joe seethed.

"Well, just eat it anyways. If you don't, I will," Johnny replied.

They started packing their gear.

"Whoa, Hank left his tent?" asked Joe.

"Ah yeah," Johnny replied, "and some space blankets. He figured he could dead head it all the way home and it would be better for us to have it."

"Huh, that's cool. I guess," Joe replied.

"Yeah, better than lying in the dirt ya know?" Johnny tried to rationalize.

"Yeah true," Joe replied. "He left his map as well? How is he gonna get home?"

"Uh, well think of this," Johnny lied, "he isn't loaded down with cocaine. He can take the main toll roads that we can't, so it's a straight shot home for him."

"Ah yeah that makes sense," Joe replied.

After they packed up all their gear, they had to figure a way to tie the pup tent to Joe's bike. Using some bungee cord they finally fixed it to the side of one of his saddle bags.

"Shit, we gottta dig up the product now," Johnny announced.

"Uh yeah, duh, the whole reason we are here." Joe face palmed himself in a jokey way. "How could I forget?"

Johnny pushed his bike over towards the tree where they had buried all their kilos. He gave the entire site a quick once over to make sure none of Hank's blood was now showing in the morning sunlight. As far as he could see there was none.

It took them another forty minutes to retrieve all their kilos and pack them back into their saddle bags. They were now ready to go.

Joe tapped his gas tank and then pulled the cap off it.

"Fuck man, I'm low on gas. I was so keen to get out of the city earlier I didn't even think to gas up."

Johnny grabbed Hank's portable gas can. "Here, this still has some motion potion in it, use this." He handed it to Joe.

"Oh wow, at least Hank left us some gas," Joe remarked. He topped up his tank and strapped the empty gas can to his other saddle bag, using another bungee cord.

The duo headed north down the old road.

CHAPTER THIRTY-SEVEN

They made slow going on the rough road. Instead of hitting sixty to seventy kilometers an hour Johnny found they were averaging about twenty-five or so. Not good as there was no sign of life, no street signs, no billboards, no cars and no people. Every couple of miles he would slow down and scan the horizon for any signs of civilization. Finally, the worst happened.

"Shit, I'm out of gas," Johnny announced.

"What about your reserve tank?" Joe asked.

"That was my reserve tank." Johnny sighed. "I was hoping for a gas station by now. Ya know?"

"Yeah, tell me about it. I am starving too," Joe added. "That protein bar just made me hungrier, if anything."

"Ahh there has got to be something soon. What do you think? Scout ahead and see if you can find a gas station?" Johnny asked.

"The problem with that," Joe replied, "is that if I ride ahead and ride back to get ya I am burning double fuel. What about I just foot push ya?"

Johnny thought for a moment. "Foot push? Shit, I haven't done that since the '80s. If you're down to try it I'm game."

"Okay, well, let's try that, at least we're heading in the right direction of home," Joe replied. "Drop your left side passenger foot peg Ace."

It took them a moment to build up momentum but soon Joe was riding right behind Johnny with his right foot on Johnny's left side passenger foot peg, propelling them both along. Soon they were moving on at a semi decent speed, Johnny estimated about thirty miles per hour. On the left side of the road Johnny spotted some more Oxen, the same ones that had gotten Hank killed. He wondered if they were wild or some farmer's stock. If so, maybe they could buy some gas from one of these farmers.

Finally, after about ten miles he heard the dreaded, "Oh no!" from Joe.

Johnny risked a look back to see Joe staring down at his tank with a shocked look on his face.

Fuck, he is out of gas! Johnny thought.

"Dude I'm done," Joe declared, coming to a slow stop. Johnny rolled ahead and put his boots down Fred Flintstone style to stop. Still no civilization in sight.

"What now?" Joe asked.

"I guess we push 'em." Johnny shrugged.

The duo hopped off and started pushing their scoots. Six hundred pounds on a dirt road? Not fun.

"This is some bullshit," Johnny exclaimed after a mile or two.

"You know what the only good thing about this is?" asked Joe.

"What?" asked Johnny.

"We ain't pushing uphill," Joe replied.

Johnny laughed. It wasn't funny but Joe was correct. The only thing worse than pushing two heavily laden baggers on a dirt road was trying to push them uphill.

"I'm gonna need a break soon," Joe announced. "I'm tired, I'm thirsty and above all I am super hungry."

"Yeah, I hear that. Let's do another mile or so," Johnny suggested. "You see that bend in the road up ahead? Let's get to there and we will stop for ten minutes."

Joe looked ahead to where Johnny was pointing. "Okay, done deal."

By the time they made it to the point in the road Johnny had suggested Joe was beat.

"Dude gimmie ten minutes to get my breath. I'm done," Joe pleaded.

"No worries man. I get it. Trust me, I do," Johnny replied. They pulled their bikes to the side of the road, just in case some crazy speeder came flying around the corner and knocked their bikes down. Then they would be truly screwed.

Johnny sat for a moment with his friend and then started feeling restless.

"Hey, I might walk up head and have a look around. You okay on waiting here alone?" Johnny asked.

Joe looked around. "Yeah, should be okay. What are ya thinking?"

"Hmm maybe ten minutes up the road and ten minutes back?" Johnny figured that might be enough to look for a farmhouse or something.

"Okay, do it," Joe replied. "I'll be here."

Johnny trudged up ahead. Once he was around the bend, he pulled his personal stash of coke out and took a couple of snorts. He wasn't sure what the combo of cocaine and dehydration would do to him (probably nothing good), but at least it would stop him being hungry.

He returned the bag to his vest pocket and kept walking the road heading north.

Johnny looked at his watch. Twelve minutes had passed. He was considering going back until he spied a bend in the road heading left. Curiosity got the better of him and he decided to walk to the next bend before returning to Joe.

He walked up to the next turn in the road and to his surprise, there was a paved road heading east and west. He knew that earlier on the same road heading east led to the edge of a cliff so he decided to investigate the left turn to the west.

Johnny walked about a half mile down the paved road and stopped and stared. He couldn't believe what he was seeing. Looked like a small town. He spied a gas station and what appeared to be a diner. He needed to make sure it wasn't abandoned before heading back to Joe with good news. So, he walked down to check it out. Sure enough, a real-life gas station and across the street and down a bit was a combo diner and general store. Not only was it a diner, it actually served beers too! They were saved.

Johnny went into the gas station and bought two ice cold cokes. He had no idea what the clerk was charging for them, so after a few minutes of sign language he handed the man a U.S. five-dollar bill. The clerk passed him back a handful of pesos. Johnny had no clue of their worth or the exchange rate. He was just happy to have found a gas station open.

He waved goodbye to the clerk and headed out with the two cold sodas. He cracked the top on his and sipped on it as he walked back. Joe would be happy with the news. Things were looking up for the duo.

CHAPTER THIRTY-EIGHT

Johnny walked back to their dirt road. He made it down the first bend only to see a figure walking towards him. It took him and second to realize it was indeed Joe.

"Hey, what are ya doing all the way up here?" he asked.

"I got bored waiting for you and was worried you might have gotten lost," Joe explained.

"Good news. I found a gas station, grabbed you a soda too," Johnny replied, tossing the glass coke bottle to Joe.

"Oh shit, thanks," said Joe, easily catching the cold soda. "Thought maybe you had fallen off a cliff or something."

Johnny faltered at that but quickly adjusted his expression. "Hey, you ain't getting rid of me that quickly." Johnny laughed as they walked back to where they left their bikes.

"So what did ya find? A big town? A city?" Joe asked.

"Nah, nothing like that, some type of one horse town that seen better days," Johnny explained.

"Ah shit, at this point as long as they got food and gas, I don't give a rat's ass," Joe replied.

"Me too," Johnny said. It took them about fifteen minutes to get back to their bikes, Without realizing it, Johnny automatically checked his saddle bags to make sure his stash was all still there. Joe didn't notice.

They then spent the next twenty minutes pushing their bikes back along the dirt road to the one horse town.

"You know we could have just walked up with Hank's gas can, topped up our tanks and ridden back?" Joe asked.

"Yeah, I thought of that," Johnny replied. "But I would have to walk there and back four times total then ride there again to properly fill our tanks. So this works okay."

"Yeah, I guess," said Joe. "Hey, you think this place will still be serving breakfast?"

"No clue brother. Mind you I am so hungry right now I would probably eat anything they served," said Johnny.

"Haha, I hear that," Joe replied.

The duo pushed their bikes the rest of the way in silence. Both were physically and mentally exhausted after the last twenty-four hours. It wasn't noon yet, but it was already starting to get very warm. Save your breath until after some food and drink was the unspoken rule for now.

When they finally got to the run-down gas station, the pair filled their tanks. Johnny topped off his oil too as it was looking a little low. He loved his Harleys, but god did they love to leak oil.

200

After paying the attendant, Joe was eager for food and drink.

"C'mon man, I'm buying," he said.

"That makes a change," joked Johnny.

They cruised over to the diner in first gear. They pulled up right out front and Joe was just getting off his scoot when Johnny suggested, "Hold on a minute, let me look 'round back."

'Oh, problems?" asked Joe.

"No, no. Well, last least not yet. The last thing we need is some local cops seeing our American plates and wanting to give us a shake down. Not good, ya know?" Johnny explained.

"Oh yeah, good thinking Ace," Joe replied.

With Joe standing guard by their bikes, Johnny took a quick walk around the side of the building. More cars were parked down the side. He went to the back and there he spied two old run down cars who had seen better days. One car looked like it hadn't run since the 1980s. They could fit both bikes in between the abandoned cars and no one coming from the North or South would spot their bikes. He hadn't spotted any kids around, so he figured their chances of some curious young boys searching their saddle bags were slim to none.

Johny returned to the front and gave Joe the thumbs up. He re-mounted his trusted Iron Horse and cruised in first gear to the back of the building. Joe followed him.

They managed to get both bikes hidden between the dilapidated cars and were satisfied they would be "fairly" safe back there. Besides, they were not planning to stay long. A quick bite to eat, some coffee, then hit the road. Who knows, they might even make it back into the good ol' USA by late tonight.

They went back to the front of the diner and entered. Johnny noticed the clock on the wall said 11:50 a.m. They had been on the go since dawn. No wonder they were hungry and thirsty. He had no clue how far they had come or how far they had to go.

He took a booth at the back of the dinner facing the door. Old habits die hard. Johnny always liked to have one eye on the door to keep a tab on an establishment's comings and goings.

Their waitress came over and handed them menus. Once again, they were going to have to point at pictures since neither of them spoke much Spanish. To Johnny's surprise their waitress Camila spoke fluent English. She had spent time studying in the USA during her high school days.

To Joe's dismay they had stopped serving breakfast at 11 a.m. *Hey, this wasn't Denny's with their all day breakfast after all.* He settled for two fully loaded burritos and

Johnny ordered steak and eggs. Despite being a rundown diner that had seen better days, the food was surprisingly good.

Sipping on coffee after they had eaten, Johnny learned from Camila that they still had about eight to nine hours of riding to go. Probably more if you factored in the dirt road versus highway riding. However, he wasn't going to tell her he was taking back roads. He saw it as a purely need-to-know basis, as far as he was concerned. She also informed them that the road the diner was on used to be the main road south to Mazatlan in the '50s and '60s. When the toll road, which was a few miles west of their location was built in the '70s, the town had withered up and died. The only reason her family had been able to keep the gas station and the diner going was a decent sized town approximately ten kilometers north of them (however far twas that in miles?) and a small farming community approximately forty kilometers south of them.

Johnny finished his coffee and decided to hit the bathroom before they made the rest of their journey home. When he returned, he was shocked to find two beers sitting on their table and Joe with a shit eating grin on his face.

"Hey, come on man. One beer then we go," Joe rationalized. "It's been a long hot morning. Who knows when we'll be able to drink a beer again. Probably not until we reach Phoenix, eh?"

"You fucker," swore Johnny. "Oh well one beer can't hurt."

He sat back down and cheersed Joe. *Dammit, he was right, an ice-cold beer tastes perfect right now.*

As they were sipping on their cold brews a few more locals came in to eat. Most seemed like farmers and short haul truckers from what Johnny could tell.

They had nearly finished their beers when Camila approached with two more. "On the house," she explained. *It would have been just rude to turn down to free beers,* Johnny reasoned.

Johnny was finally starting to loosen up. Food in his belly, some coffee and now beers. Things were on the up and up. Screw it, even if they didn't make it back tonight, they could sleep out under the stars one more night and make it back home to Phoenix at first light. Besides, he was going to have to cross his buddy's ranch to get into the USA; he was going to need to see where he was going to do so.

"We will hit the road after this," Johnny declared, holding his beer bottle in the air to show Joe how much he had left.

"Works for me," Joe replied. "You think we'll make it home tonight?"

"Eh, probably first light tomorrow, bro," Johnny said.

"Cool," Joe replied.

The lunch time crowd was now starting to thin out. As an old habit, Johnny kept one eye on the door at all times. He was down to the last couple of swigs of beer, and they would be following the lunch timers out the door too.

In the midst of explaining to Joe how they had to approach his friend's border-based ranch the door swung open. Four large bikers swaggered into the diner. Despite being some distance from Joe and Johnny's booth, Johnny easily spied the "One percenter" diamond patches on their riding vests.

"Hey Joe, Joe." Johnny tried to subtly get his friend's attention. "Some bikers just walked in. You recognize the club?"

Joe tried to peer back at the bikers from the side of their booth. He caught the last two club members sitting down with their backs to the duo. He caught a quick flash of their three-piece club colors.

"Hmm might be the Dark Legion," Joe surmised.

"The Dark Legion MC? Who the fuck are they?" Johnny asked.

"Started in Utah or Idaho, I think," explained Joe. "Then made their way down to Northern Arizona."

"Never heard of them," Johnny replied.

"If it is indeed them, they are a long way from home," Joe added.

"Maybe there's a run on that we're not aware of," suggested Johnny.

"Yeah possibly," Joe replied.

"Well, the end of the day we can't leave now," Johnny stated.

"Why? I'm nearly done with my beer," Joe moaned.

"Cuz it shows weakness. That's why," Johnny explained. "We will order one last round then we go."

"Oh, okay that works for me." Joe smiled.

"Yeah, just cradle it. Take your time with it. No need to chug it. We will leave after that," Johnny suggested.

He signaled their waitress Camila to bring them two more beers and continued his conversation with Joe. He made a mental note that more of the lunch time crowd were filtering out. Were they genuinely planning to leave at that time or did the Outlaw Bikers scare them off?

CHAPTER THIRTY-NINE

Joe got up to hit the restroom. Camila bought over two more beers.

"Friends of yours?" she asked nodding back towards the four newcomers.

"Never seen them before in my life," Johnny replied.

"Oh okay, thought they might have been friends of yours," Camila replied before heading back to the diner's kitchen.

As Joe returned from the bathroom he declared to Johnny, "Well one of them just gave me a friendly nod. Does that mean we can leave now?"

"Nah nah, that just means they've seen us. We still gotta give it time before we walk out," Johnny explained. "We can't let them think we are leaving because of them."

"Aright, fair enough," Joe replied. "I've got another cold beer, so all good."

One of the younger bikers walked past Joe and Johnny on his way to the bathroom. Johnny did his best to make a quick assessment of the younger biker just as he was sure the man was doing to him. He gave Johnny a quick nod as he passed by. Johnny returned the nod.

Soon as the man entered the restroom, Joe nodded. "Yep, Dark Legion."

Johnny didn't say anything, just nodded solemnly.

Moments later the man returned. He slowed as he passed them heading back towards his booth. At the last moment he stopped and came back to their booth.

"You guys ride?" he asked.

"Yeah, we do in fact," Joe replied.

"I knew it! You look like bikers," the man explained. "But no bikes?"

"Not today," Johnny added quickly, waiting for the man to return to his friends.

"You look familiar," the stranger continued. "You ride for a club?"

"Not anymore," Johnny replied, not wanting to give Joe a chance to over share information.

"I've definitely met you both before," the stranger stated. "Just can't think where."

"Sorry bud, you don't look familiar," Johnny replied, trying to get the biker to leave them and return to his table.

"Oh well, I'm sure it will come to me," the man said. "Safe travels." He walked off to rejoin his buddies.

After the younger biker left, joe turned to Johnny, "I don't recognize him, do you?"

"Nah, never seen him before," Johnny replied. "Let's finish these, pay up our tab and get the hell out of here."

"Yeah, I get ya," said Joe, eying his beer bottle.

Before they even had a chance to finish the stranger returned carrying three more bottles of beer. Without asking, he slid into the booth next to Joe and placed the beers on the table.

"Hey, I never introduced myself before, I'm Kyle," the stranger explained.

"Hey, I'm Joe and that is Johnny, although most people call him Ace," said Joe, holding out his hand to shake.

"Ace eh?" said Kyle. "Like the Motorhead song, Ace of Spades?"

"Yeah, something like that," Johnny replied, still suspicious of the newcomer.

"So you boys on vacation?" Joe asked Kyle, who was still eyeing Johnny.

"Yeah, something like that, on a run to Sinaloa to meet some friends," Kyle explained.

"Ah cool, nice place," Joe said. Johnny held eye contact with Kyle who was still more interested in Johnny than Joe's small talk.

"How about you guys?" Kyle asked Joe.

"Just visiting old friends," Johnny said, not giving Joe a chance to reply. The last thing Johnny wanted was to give any indication of where they had been and where they were headed.

"So this run you are on, just the four of you or is the rest of the club following too?" asked Johnny, trying to put the focus back on to Kyle.

"Just us for now..." Kyle trailed off. Johnny suspected there was more to the story, but he wasn't going to fish. Just the man's non-answer was enough to read between the lines and figure out there was much more going on.

"Well, nice meeting ya Kyle, and thanks for the beers," Johnny said, trying to subtly get rid of the newcomer.

Kyle got up to leave. "No problem fellas." He started to walk off. *Good, go. On your way fella,* Johnny thought to himself.

No sooner had he finished thinking than Kyle stopped and turned around.

"Hey you guys should join us, come meet the boys," he suggested.

"Ah thanks, but maybe some other time," Johnny said, trying to be as polite as possible but dismissive at the same time.

"Ah c'mon, I just bought you some beers, come meet the boys," Kyle insisted.

Joe, without thinking, got up, "Sure. C'mon Ace."

Stupid fuck, thought Johnny. *He's always been naive.*

Johnny had no choice now but to get up and follow Joe and Kyle over to the biker's booth.

"Hey, shift over guys," Kyle instructed his mates in the front booth. "We got some genuine O.G.s with us."

"Oh shit, nice," said the chubbiest of the four bikers, sliding down on the booth bench seat.

Joe sat down beside Kyle with his back to the door and Johnny slid in on the opposite side of the table facing the door.

Kyle introduced his friends. Mike was the chubby guy sitting by the window and on Johnny's side of the table was Frank, who looked like he worked out five times a week, and Brendan who was rocking a lumberjack's beard. Names really didn't matter as Johnny was sure he would forget them in approximately one minute.

"So what club did you ride for?" asked the chubby guy.

"Eh, we're out now so it doesn't really matter. Does it?" Johnny replied calmly.

"Oh, okay..." The Chubby guy looked dejected.

CHAPTER FORTY

Joe thought back to growing up with Johnny. They had first met in Junior High, which was weird as they only lived a few blocks from each other. They would ride bicycles all over town as kids, always exploring. Soon as they were out of school, they would go on adventures, only coming home when it got dark and it was time to eat dinner with their respective families. No cell phones in those days. You could get away with just about anything back then. On the weekends they would ride even further.

It was Johnny who got Joe into customizing his bicycle. Where Johnny learned this knowledge, he had no idea. This was a long, long time before the internet. How was this knowledge passed down? Word of mouth, Joe guessed. Anyways, Johnny turned up one day he had a banana seat, a sissy bar, high rise handlebars and an extended front fork. Bad ass. Joe begged Johnny to help him customize his bike too and pretty soon, they were wrenching every weekend to get Joe's bike to the same level of cool as Johnny's.

One day they were riding on a Sunday afternoon in an industrial area–back in the late '70s an industrial area in

Tucson on Sunday afternoon would be deserted. No people to be seen for miles and miles. However, this Sunday was different; three dirty looking hippy types were working on their Chopper motorcycles out front of some old warehouse. They saw the boys approaching and waved at them.

"Hey kids, cool bikes," one of the hippies greeted them.

"Wow, your bikes are cool," Joe replied, having never seen Chopper motorcycles in real life before, not realizing that the "hippies" they were talking to were actual real-life bikers.

"Wanna try it?" the man offered. At first, Joe thought he meant take it for a ride (no way!) but then he realized he just wanted him to twist the throttle. He eagerly agreed. From that afternoon on Johnny and Joe were determined to get their own Motorcycles as soon as they turned sixteen.

By the end of the 1970s BMX was replacing cruiser bicycles as the most popular bikes and that was Joe or Johnny's scene. Pretty soon they both owned used Honda NS 125 cc bikes which they rode everywhere. Joe always felt they were great beginners' bikes for him and Johnny: cheap, reliable and rarely, if ever, broke down. All you had to do was remember to change the oil every 7000 miles or so and you were good to go. Despite being metric bikes, the little scoots got Joe and Johnny started on a lifetime of wrenching. Overnight, they went from nerds in the crowd to cool guys. Girls wanted after school rides on them and the other guys in their high school classes wanted to buy their own too. Life was good.

Out of high school and their first "adult jobs", they both bought used Harleys. 883 Sportsters. Power wise it was not a big deal but upscaling from little Hondas they felt like they owned the universe. The used Harleys were much less reliable than their little Hondas and their education on working on their scoots begun in earnest.

Since they were both working full-time and living at home, the pair had plenty of money for going out on the weekends. Unfortunately, that was the year Regan made changes to the law to make it twenty-one to drink. Fortunately, they would hit dive bars that they knew didn't ID them, or didn't care. They soon became familiar faces at most of the biker bars around town. The older biker women (who in hindsight were probably only thirty years old at the time) took a shine to them and soon they both had their pick and choose of the finest biker gals in Tucson.

Around the same time as they were hitting the bars every weekend Johnny got approached at work (of all places) to prospect for the Steel Reapers, the premier bike club in Arizona at that time. Of course, he said yes and after one year of running around doing everything and anything a fully patched member of the reapers told him to do, Johnny became a club member. He lobbied hard for Joe to join too and soon Joe was maintaining the Reapers Tuscon clubhouse, cleaning and detailing the guys' bikes, fetching burgers for them and pretty much anything else that was required of him. Six months later he was patched in as well. The proudest day of his life.

Them joining the club saw them travel over pretty much all of the lower forty-eight states in the coming years. Getting older and wiser somewhere along the way, they traded their hard tail choppers for fancy dressers bikes that didn't ruin the backs after ten miles of hard riding. Sure they had "dad" bikes now, but what the heck, they earned that right as far as Joe was concerned.

When Johnny left the club after nearly forty years, Joe had followed suit. The old guard were either all dead or in jail doing serious prison time. First they were both out good with the club but a month later Johnny was told he was now out bad and not to contact or hang around any current members from now on, or there would be "problems". That had stung but Joe had learned to live with it. He wasn't quite sure why Johnny was out bad and he was out good, but it was what it was. What was the saying, "All good things come to an end?" Something like that.

He had to get up to piss again. Once he was up, he figured he would settle up their check with Camila while he was at it. That way soon as they were finished with their beers they could just leave. Nothing worse than trying to track down your waitress and she was nowhere to be found.

When Joe had paid the check and returned from the restroom, Johnny got up to take a piss too. In the stall he realized he was starting to get a buzz on. Lack of food and water, plus a bunch of drinks, he assumed was the culprit in feeling buzzed so soon. It then dawned on him he was still carrying the free stash Momo had supplied them with back in Copala. Johnny took a couple of snorts to straighten himself out before returning to the younger bikers' booth.

Kyle nodded at him when he sat back down.

"So this is an official club run?" asked Johnny.

The four Dark Legion riders looked at each before deciding to answer. "Yeah, something like that," Kyle lied.

If Johnny was to assume, he figured they had come down to Mexico to make a drug buy or connect maybe with or without the approval of the rest of their club.

"Cool," Johnny replied, playing along with their deception.

Kyle got up and announced to the table, "Just stepping outside for a smoke." He held up what appeared to be a joint and not a cigarette.

Fair enough, thought Johnny.

Joe and Johnny made small talk with the other guys until Kyle returned. He sat back down next to Joe and opposite

Johnny. Looking directly in Johnny's eyes, he stated, "No bikes."

"Huh?" asked Johnny.

"There are no bikes out there and no cars," Kyle elaborated. "There are no cars in the car park, so how did you get here?"

"Oh, they're back by the gas station, across the street," Johnny lied. These fools didn't need to know where their bikes were hidden.

"Ah, makes sense," Kyle said. He was still looking directly at Johnny.

"Ace McIntire, you don't remember me, do you?" Kyle asked.

How the fuck does he know my last name? Johnny thought to himself.

CHAPTER FORTY-ONE

I told you before, I've never seen you before in my life," Johnny replied.

"You have though," Kyle continued. "The name Bill Ossi mean anything to you?"

Johnny thought for a moment. "No, not at all."

"Wild Bill from the Daggered Souls Motorcycle club?"

Wild Bill *did* ring a bell. "Hmm, maybe Wild Bill. Out of Nevada right?"

"No, Idaho," Kyle corrected. "You see Bill Ossi is my dad. My name is Kyle Ossi."

"Okay, and?" Johnny asked.

The other Dark Legion guys started to stiffen. They could feel the tension in the air. Johnny wasn't sure where this was heading.

"About eighteen years ago, we met on an inter club run, in Laughlin," Kyle explained.

"Sorry kid, I went on a lot of runs for a lot of years, I can't remember them all," Johnny replied.

"Well, I remember this one," Kyle continued. "I was twelve. My dad took me on that run. My first run."

"Very cool," Johnny commented.

"Well, it was cool." Kyle paused for effect. "It was a cool run, until you beat the shit out of my dad and put him in the hospital. How cool was that?"

Johnny cast his mind back. He had been in so many fights, so much inter club drama over the years, it was all a giant blur, something that he had put behind him in recent years.

"Well sorry to hear it kid," Johnny replied. "If I did do that. One, I don't remember and two, if I did put him in hospital, I probably had a damn good reason for it."

"That's not what he told me," Kyle replied. "Said it was some stupid beef over a spilled beer or something."

"Okay," Johnny said, knowing damn well a lot of people who lose fights will lie and say, "Oh they sucker punched me" or "His four buddies jumped in and pack ratted me" just to save face.

"You ruined his life. He was never the same after that," Kyle continued.

"Well, I'm not saying I did beat your dad up Kyle," Johnny responded. "But any time you fight someone in the street, things can go wrong. Heck, I've known guys to hit someone one time, the person falls back, hits the back of their head and dies. That's one of the inherent dangerous of street fighting."

"Fuck you, liar," Kyle said.

Everyone stopped what they were doing.

"Hey kid, just stop. You say this was twenty years ago. I have no recollection of it. Let Joe up and we will get going."

"No," Kyle replied. "You fucks ain't going anywhere. Except, to the hospital!"

"Nah. We're leaving," Johnny stated.

"Come one tough guy, you and me, let's fight," Kyle challenged Johnny.

"I'm not fighting you kid, I gotta be thirty years older than you," Johnny replied.

"Get up chicken shit," Kyle challenged.

Johnny was in no mood for this, Too much at stake. He just wanted to leave, grab his bike, get back on that dirt road and head home. Last thing he wanted was to be riding with a busted-up face, hands or body.

"Listen sonny. I've already killed someone in the last twenty-four hours, no problem for me to make it two people. So just let Joe get up and we will be on our way," Johnny stated.

"Bullshit," Kyle hissed. "Come on, let's fight." He stood up and started to squeeze out of the booth.

At that moment, Johnny pulled his Glock from his waistband and shot Kyle point blank in the chest. The noise of the gun fire made everything seem to unfold in slow motion.

As Kyle fell back, Joe had the presence of mind to push him out of the booth. Kyle's lifeless body crashed to the diner floor.

CHAPTER FORTY-TWO

Johnny seized the moment and, in all the confusion, jumped up before Kyle's friends could grab him. He swung the pistol 'round on the remaining Dark Legion bikers.

"Don't even think about it," Johnny threatened. "Joe, come on, we are leaving."

The pair headed for the door. Johnny kept the gun pointed at the stunned remaining bikers.

After they exited the diner, Johnny stood in the doorway with the pistol trained on the Dark Legion riders.

"Quick, slash their tires," Johnny instructed Joe. "Then go back and get your bike started."

Joe pulled his knife and hurriedly stabbed each of their rear tires. After finishing he raced around to the back of the diner. Moments later, he could hear a scoot starting up. *Good,* thought Johnny. Soon Joe pulled around out front.

"Here, grab this," he instructed Joe, handing him his pistol. "Don't let anyone through that door."

He could see Kyle's friends looking out the front windows, shocked at the sight of Joe on his Harley.

Johnny raced around the back of the diner and quickly started his bike and pulled to the front to join his old friend.

He went to say something to Joe and could hear police sirens coming from the North. Someone at the diner must have called the cops.

"South, quick," Johnny instructed.

"But we're meant to be going north!" Joe questioned.

'We can circle back later," Johnny replied. "Time to leave!"

The pair pulled out of the diner car park kicking up dirt and rocks as they went. Johnny risked a look back to see Kyle's three friends run out of the diner.

He didn't stick around to find out if they were armed.

CHAPTER FORTY-THREE

Joe and Johnny raced south on the paved road. Johnny was keeping one eye out for pursuing law enforcement and one eye out on a potential left turn that would get them off this road and back to the dirt road running parallel to this one. He figured it had to be at least a couple of miles in from this road, but the question was how could they re-connect to it?

So far, they had just passed farms and private houses. They needed an isolated area to make the turn off without locals ratting them out to the pursuing cops. Johnny tried to do some quick math as they rode. The waitress said the next town south was about forty kilometers away. From memory that was a little over twenty-five miles away. Riding at seventy-five miles per hour meant they would be on that town in no more than twenty minutes.

Ideally, they would need to find a discreet turn off in the next ten minutes, especially if they were more cops arriving from the South. Johnny couldn't be sure, but he had to assume the worst outcome (cops coming from the South) as opposed to the best outcome of Cops only chasing them from the North. Time was not on their side. They needed a break, and they needed one fast.

Of course, there was the slight possibility that the Dark Legion club guys wouldn't rat them out to the police and aim to deal with the shooting on club terms. But Johnny's faith in new school bikers and a "no snitching" policy wasn't big. He figured guys like that would roll over right away and roadblocks would soon be set up. *Fuck, where could they turn off?*

Finally, they got a break. A dirt road straddled between two properties, Johnny pulled ahead of Joe and waved wildly, signaling him to slow down for a turn off. Johnny blipped his throttle, and he changed down quickly between gears. Even so, his back tire slid out just a fraction making the turn, instinctively tightening his sphincter, waiting for a high side smash that never came.

They rode the dirt trail for a good five miles before they figured they were close to their original dirt road that ran north to south. The problem now was a solid chain link fence blocking them from joining the road. Johnny figured the smart thing to do would be to head north run parallel to their road as much as they could till they found a break in the fence or something.

They rode over fields of hard grass, dirt and scrub, often a combination of all three. The impact of the shoddy terrain played havoc on his back and neck, but he didn't care. He could get all the chiropractic adjustments and full body massages he wanted the moment he made it back safely to the good ol' US of A. For now, getting as much distance between him, the Dark Legion Motorcycle club and local law enforcement was the name of the game.

After a mile or two of rough road Joe started waving at Johnny. The pair slowed down as Johnny saw what Joe had been waiving at. A crude gate in the fence that they could pass through. Obviously a farmer used it to control his livestock as it wasn't locked but pulled shut by a rope any child could slip off (but not a cow, goat or horse). They hopped off their bikes and ran to the gate. Joe un-slipped the rope and Johnny pulled the gate back.

They couldn't see their road in the current position; however, they both knew it was close enough to them since they had been following it all the way up. They would have to push their bikes through the last twenty, thirty feet of scrub to return to the abandoned roadway.

Soon as they had pushed their bikes past the gate Johnny ran back, pulled the gate shut and slung the rope back over the fence post. No sense letting the farm's animals run off, Johnny figured.

After pushing through the thick scrub and nearly losing balance once or twice they finally rejoined the dirt road that Johnny was confident they had travelled up earlier in the day. In fact, he saw bike tracks that had to be theirs. Good, they were on the right track. They took off north again, riding as fast as they dared on the soft dirt.

After a few miles, they came to the bends in the road where they had stopped for a break that very morning. After cruising slowly through the bends, sure enough there was the road that would lead them back to the diner and gas station. They peered down that road and couldn't see or hear anything. They then waited a minute just to be sure no one was coming for them and quickly shot over the intersecting road and back to their north-south path which would lead them home towards the USA.

Things were looking good. Was Johnny worried that the local cops might search this road at some point? He wasn't convinced, but he sure as hell wanted to get as much distance between him and the diner as possible just in case.

He needed to piss after all those afternoon beers, but Johnny wanted to make sure they were well past the small town that was north of the diner and gas station before even thinking of pulling over. He estimated a good five to ten miles further up the road should see them clear, even though he had no clue what the name of this town was, it's size or location. All of his intel was down to the say so of a friendly waitress. He had to assume it was close enough to the diner that police dispatched to a fight there could be heard in the distance in the matter of time it took them to leave the diner, ruin the bikers' tires, fetch their bikes and peel out. A few more miles should suffice before he could stop and drain the ol' lizard.

CHAPTER FORTY-FOUR

Joe trailed behind Johnny's scoot as they headed up their abandoned dirt road to freedom. He thought back to all the impossible situations that him and Ace had been through together over the years that they had somehow survived.

He laughed to himself as he thought back to a Chopper fest called Iron Horizons that he and Johnny had attended in Scottsdale, Arizona about twenty-two years back. They had only just pulled into the car park where local law enforcement informed them that their local rivals "The Blood Forged Tribe MC" were in attendance and out for blood. The cop explained to Johnny and Joe that they, law enforcement, were heavily outnumbered and if they insisted on attending with their Steel Reapers colors there was nothing the cops could do to protect them.

Johnny and Joe laughed it off, as if they were going to fall for that cop's scare tactics. They were proud of being Steel Reapers and didn't back down from anyone. Had they fought three on one, four on one before? Of course. Even then they had sent their enemies running. Besides, where could they stash their vests on their bikes? Nowhere.

It was time to nut up or shut up and hell or high water they were going to the bike fest.

They went to will call and collected their wrist bands– they were guests of one of the featured bike builders that year. They entered the main pavilion for the Chopper Fest and spent the first hour checking out the multitude of vendors in attendance, anything from biker T-shirts to those German helmets everyone was rocking back then to self-defense weapons. All in all, a good time.

They left the main pavilion and went to check out the food options. That's when the trouble started. At first there were a few guys giving them the stink eye. Then a few comments. As they went to investigate the different burger food trucks all of a sudden, they had three fully patched Blood Forged Tribe following them. Three on two? Both Joe and Johnny had faced tougher odds and won before, so they were cautious but not overly worried.

They finally found a burger food truck that looked promising and put in orders for burgers, fries and two sodas. The chick behind the counter passed Johnny two cans of sodas and gave them a ticket for their burgers. Wait time was supposed to be about five minutes.

"You've got a lot of nerve showing your faces here," the biggest of the three Blood Forged Tribe riders hissed, getting in Johnny's face.

"You've got a lot of nerve showing that face in public, you ugly bastard," Johnny replied.

Joe noticed one of the Blood Forged guys stifling a laugh at that.

"What did you say?" sneered the leader.

"Oh, ugly AND deaf?" teased Johnny. "A winning combination. I said you were UGLY you dumb prick."

The leader pulled back his arm to take a swing at Johnny. Before he had even got his shoulder all the way back, Johnny cracked him with a powerful upper cut holding his coke can. The man fell backwards, stunned as the sticky soda spurted everywhere.

Without missing a beat, Joe swung on the guy who was stifling a laugh moments before. Johnny grabbed the third man, pulling him towards Johnny then tripping him at the last second, sending him backwards on to his downed buddy. Joe's man broke free of his grip and ran off calling for help.

Joe figured that was their signal to leave, burgers be damned.

"Hey, we should leave," Joe shouted. "More will be coming."

Johnny nodded in agreement, realizing there wasn't going to be time to get their food order. They headed down another aisle of food trucks back towards the main pavilion. They hadn't gone more than fifty feet before Joe heard someone behind them announce, "There they are!" He turned back to spy at least twenty to twenty-five of the biggest, meanest looking bikers you had ever seen in your life following them.

Johnny had seen them too. Just for a moment, Joe could see Johnny contemplating making a stand. Steel Reapers had a reputation for never backing down no matter the odds. Win or lose, it didn't matter as long as you gave it your all. However, in this situation, "your all" could mean your life. Time to leave; not worth the risk.

The duo moved forwards, not running yet but definitely picking up the pace from earlier.

They were no more than forty feet from the end of the food trucks when another group of Blood Forged Legion bikers appeared in front of them.

"Quick, down here," Johnny said, grabbing Joe by his flannel shirt. He dragged them down a small gap between two sets of food trucks. "Watch the cables and wires," Johnny yelped. They moved quickly, nearly tripping over a couple of times on various cables and power outlets. They finally made it through to the other side, emerging in an aisle running parallel to their last one.

Joe looked back away from the pavilion to spy yet another group of Blood Forged Tribe bikers searching for them. These guys had butcher's cleavers and axe handles in their hands. Luckily a lot of the attendees were now surging their way too in a panic. Perfect for Johnny and Joe to blend in with.

By mixing in with the fleeing crowd they managed to get their way back into the main pavilion. Joe figured crisis averted, those dummies will still be searching the food trucks for them. No sooner had he thought that when he heard a shout, "There they are." He looked up to see a group of five Blood Forged Tribe dudes sitting in the arena seats making their way towards them. If they didn't move now, these guys would be on them in a minute.

Just as Joe was pushing Johnny ahead, he heard another shout, "That's them by the leather booth." That was coming from behind them. Back where they had just entered from outside. They pushed forwards, towards the main entrance and exit.

They rounded another corner of vendors only to run smack bang into two more Blood Forged Tribe guys searching for them. No time to stop and fight them, Johnny pushed his man out of the way and Joe kicked out at the legs of one thug nearest to him, catching him in the shin and taking his legs out from under him. The man went down, and Joe and Johnny were now starting to move at a near running pace.

As they made the main doors, Joe dared a look back; there were bikers coming at them from the side and the main concourse of the exhibitor's pavilion. It was hard to tell but it looked like hundreds of men coming at them. Way, way more than they had expected.

He grabbed Johnny and pulled him through the glass doors.

"Bro, we gotta hoof it. There are hundreds of them!" he shouted at Johnny.

They started their way through the massive car park filled with bikes, thousands of them. Joe was confident they were heading in the right direction. Joe risked another look back, hundreds of bikers were swarming out of the main building, all cheering and shouting. *No way can they all be Blood Forged Tribe riders*, Joe thought, *no way.*

"We're gonna have to come back for our bikes," Johnny shouted. "We're not going to have time to get to them."

Joe thought about it for a second. Ace was right—by the time they jumped onto their bikes they would be swarmed. Already some of the younger guys had made it to the outskirts of the car park.

Someone started firing at them. Joe felt a bullet whiz by his ear. He ducked down between two cars and started bear crawling away from the oncoming swarm of angry outlaws. Johnny was doing the same.

They soon found themselves at the edge of the event center's car park. Open fields to their right and the 101 freeway to their left.

"The freeway!" Johnny shouted.

"We don't have a car!' Joe shouted back.

"Just shut up and run," Johnny replied.

They raced towards the usually busy freeway. Johnny was slightly ahead of Joe and had reached the concrete retaining wall and pulled himself over.

Are we really doing this? Joe questioned for a moment, before two bullets peppered the ground to his right. *Uh, I guess we are!* He grabbed the wall and flung himself over.

They found themselves on the hard shoulder for the fast lane, with cars speeding by at seventy plus miles per hour, inches from them. Johnny held his right arm over Joe's chest in a "stay back" gesture.

Johnny waited until there was a gap in the traffic. "Okay, now!" he shouted at Joe as they sprinted over the four-lane southbound highway.

The duo pulled themselves up and over the next concrete retaining wall to find themselves in a little oasis between the southbound and northbound sides of the freeway. It seemed if they walked north, they could actually avoid having to cross the northbound side of the 101.

Joe's lungs were burning from all the running plus the adrenalin dump. They slowly made their way down the little no man's land path between the two sections of the 101 freeway and found their way to a little strip mall. There was a welcoming neon sign of a Applebee's type restaurant in the shopping complex and Joe and Johnny made a bee line there.

"I never got my burger dammit," Johnny explained, pulling open the doors of the food joint. "I could do with a beer too."

The hostess offered to sit them near the bar, but Johnny insisted on a booth at the back, with him naturally facing the front door. They ordered a couple of beers and burgers and sipped on their drinks while waiting for their food to be served.

Joe was halfway through his burger when Johnny hissed, "Shit! Duck down."

Joe hunched over in their booth, as did Johnny.

After a moment he propped himself back up in his seat.

"Fuck they are STILL looking for us! What the hell man?" he exclaimed.

Joe looked back towards the front door but couldn't see anyone.

"How did they co-ordinate so fast?" Joe asked his buddy.

"My theory," Johnny replied, "is those damn cell phones. Everyone's got one now. I reckon they used those to rally the troops and hunt us down."

Joe thought on that for a moment–he knew some people had cell phones. But outlaw bikers? That many of them? Maybe Johnny was on to something.

"Yeah, I'm thinking you might be right. The moment they bring down prices I might get one too," Joe replied.

"Ehh, it's probably just a fad," Johnny replied dismissively. "As long as I have a quarter in my pocket I can always find a pay phone. Besides, I heard they gouge you if you go over your limit on texting before 7 p.m., fuck that shit. I have enough bills as it is without paying out 200 bucks a month for a phone I might use a few times a week."

"Yeah, true," Joe replied. "What are we gonna do about our bikes?"

Johnny thought on this for a moment. If they left after hours, would theirs be the only two bikes in the lot, making them easy to spot? Would the club leave scouts behind to wait for them? Maybe their best course of action would be to leave their colors somewhere safe, return to the fest , collect their bikes and come back and grab their colors?

"Okay, just an idea. What about this," Johnny explained, "we dump our colors, maybe you take your flannel off too. We go back grab our bikes and then swing back and grab our colors."

"Why not just go after the event shuts down for the night?" Joe asked.

"Well then it becomes clear that's our bikes and we are sitting targets. We don't know if they will have people still waiting," said Johnny.

"Yeah, smart," Joe replied. "What if we leave our colors here, maybe with that waitress and cab it over?" Joe suggested. "We would look like new arrivals?"

"Yeah, I like it, let me go speak to our waitress and see if she can call us a cab too," said Johnny.

Johnny's plan had worked. Their kind waitress let them stow their club colors and Joe's flannel behind the counter. They cabbed it back over to the Chopper festival, acted like completely different people, grabbed their bikes and headed back to the restaurant to collect their belongings. Joe did notice a bunch of prospects lurking around the car park eyeballing them and other attendees, but luckily there were so many other bikers coming and going they didn't realize the men they were looking for passed right in front of their noses.

As they were ready to leave the restaurant, Joe turned to Johnny and asked, "Hey, how did this feud with the Blood Forged Tribe MC even start?"

Johnny thought for a moment. "Honestly, I don't really know. Over two women, I wanna say, but back in the late '60s early '70s."

"Isn't it always over a woman?" Joe asked.

"Pretty much." Johnny shrugged, pulling on his helmet and firing up his scoot.

Joe had been surprised they had survived that night. In those days he was always down for a good fight but up against those numbers, it would have been a massacre. Their massacre. Years later, a peace treaty between both clubs was brokered and guys you would have once had to bash on sight would now give you a courteous nod if you ran into them at a bike night or a swap meet.

CHAPTER FORTY-FIVE

Joe looked up to see Johnny signaling for them to pull over. He had found a spot with a wide enough shoulder to pull over without being run down if some locals tried to race up their road at top speed. Joe surmised that perhaps it was once a spot to pull off the road for some sightseeing, maybe a picnic? Either way, there was enough room for a few cars to park and be well clear of the "roadway" beside them.

Joe nodded that he understood and geared down to a stop.

"I gotta piss," Johnny announced after pulling off his helmet.

"Yeah, same," added Joe. "All those beers went right through me."

Joe wandered off into the scrub near enough to Johnny so they could communicate if needed but not close enough to make it weird.

When they returned to their bikes Joe asked Johnny, "Any idea where we are?"

"Well, that waitress said there was a small town a few miles north of them," Johnny explained. "I think we gotta be ten miles or so north of that but running parallel to them."

"Ah okay," Joe replied, still not sure what that meant for their travel time to cross the border.

"Let me check the map Hank left us," Johnny continued.

"Okay, cool," Joe replied.

Johnny studied the map. He then studied it some more, when it suddenly occurred to Joe that it was weird that Hank would leave his map, his gas can and his camping tent with them. *Surely, he needed those items himself to get home?*

"Well? How we looking?" Joe asked, sick of waiting.

"Ahh not sure without GPS, hard to tell. But at a guess I would say we have about four hours to Santa Ana."

"Santa Ana, California? We don't want to be anywhere near California," Joe exclaimed.

"No dumb ass! Santa Ana in Sonora," Johnny corrected him.

"How was I to know there was two of them?" Joe asked.

Johnny shook his head. "I say we ride for another hour or so and then set up camp before it gets too dark. We can cross the border and be back home tomorrow morning."

"Great, can't wait," Joe replied.

Neither rider was especially keen to get back on their scoots at this point. The sun was starting to go down, it had been a crazy twenty-four hours for both of them and now they riding further north to try and find a suitable spot to pull over for the night.

Finally, Johnny announced, "Well, I guess we should get going."

"Yeah, sounds good," Joe replied, walking back toward his Harley. "Hey, I got a question for ya."

"Yeah, what's up?" asked Johnny.

"Back at the diner when you were dealing with the Dark Legions guy," Joe started.

"Okay..."

"You mentioned to them you had already killed someone today," Joe continued. "Do you mean Hank?"

"What? Ahh…" Johnny was red faced. "Uhhh, no."

"I just think it's weird that...."

"Are you fucking accusing me of killing the old man?" Johnny raged. "How fucking dare you!"

"I just think it's weird that he would have left his tent, gas can and maps with us," Joe stated, taken back by Johnny's reaction to his line of questioning.

"Right, that is it," Johnny snarled, rhino charging Joe with full aggression. Joe barely had time to raise his arms before Johnny was on him. Grabbing the collar of his leather jacket with his left hand he hammered blows down on Joe's face. Joe staggered backwards partly in shock, partly because one of Johnny's punches hit that special button on your jaw that was known to send you unconscious.

Falling backwards, he fell out of Johnny's grasp and earned himself a temporary reprieve from the flurry of punches Johnny had unleashed on him. Still, Joe was struggling to stay alert, especially from that one punch that had rocked him hard.

Before he had a chance to clear the cobwebs in his brain, Johnny had lept on Joe's back and wrapped one of his thick muscular arms around Joe's neck. He could feel the life being squeezed out of him. He recalled once a pro fighter telling him that you pretty much had fifteen to twenty seconds to react before you lost consciousness from a choke hold like this. Joe had to do something, and fast.

He reached down for his boot knife. However, his right leg was twisted up behind him and he couldn't manage. Joe could feel himself fading into black. Bringing his right hand up from his failed attempt to retrieve his boot knife, he felt the pistol Johnny had passed to him when they had fought their way out of the diner. In all the excitement earlier, he had forgotten he hadn't given it back to Johnny. He pulled it from his waistband and with his last bit of consciousness, he reached past his left side and fired it into Johnny's center body mass. Johnny yelped and let go.

241

Joe rolled to his right and brought Johnny's gun up, more instinctively than anything else. A defensive reaction? Muscle memory? Survival?

"You shot me, you fuck, you shot me!" Johnny yelled and then proceeded to come at Joe again. Without thinking, Joe fired again and again into his oldest friend until the man went down. Adrenaline is a hell of a drug.

Johnny lay in the dirt, writhing in agony. Joe scrambled to his feet, still trying to get his brain in gear. The repeated blows to the face and getting choked out had messed him up, badly.

Johnny stopped thrashing about in the dirt. Joe kept his distance, still attempting to come to grips with what had just happened. He had killed his best friend. Correction, no, he had killed the guy who was trying to kill him. A guy who was once his best friend. His best friend, who had killed Hank.

All of a sudden Joe got terribly paranoid. He looked around. Were there witnesses? What if the cops arrived now and caught him with the gun in his hand? He didn't want to spend the rest of his life doing hard time in a Mexican prison. Joe's instinct was to just leave now and fast. He thought about just leaving but Johnny's Harley lying out in the open like that would be noticed by the very first farmer that rode by. Could he risk it? Joe thought better and decided to wheel it over the small embankment nearby. He hated to do that to a perfectly good Harley, but he couldn't think of what else to do at this moment.

Joe looked over at Johnny's bike. He then pulled Hank's gas can and the paper map from it before wiping it down of any fingerprints he might have left on it. After pulling on his riding gloves, he jumped on Johnny's ride and kicked the bike into gear, riding as close to the edge as he dared before dismounting and rolling it down the hill. The bike made it about halfway down before tipping over on its side and coming to an undignified stop. Joe felt bad for doing so but he was now in self-preservation mode.

He contemplated leaving Johnny's body where it lay but even though he had killed Hank he still loved his dead brother and knew he had to bury him. He scoured the area and found a branch that was sturdy enough to bust up the dirt and help him start digging a make-shift grave for Johnny.

After an hour of digging, he had made a deep enough hole to bury his best friend. Joe decided to remove Johnny's wallet and rings. If his body was ever found he would hope the local cops figured it was a robbery gone wrong and investigate locally. He dragged Johnny over and rolled him into the makeshift grave. He felt terrible but then again, Johnny had killed old man Hank. That guy didn't deserve to be put down like that. Joe also reminded himself that Johnny was trying to kill him too, which he probably would have done if Joe hadn't still had Johnny's Glock.

It was now too late to ride; he would have to stay here for the night, which gave him the creeps. Joe also realized that he should have probably pulled Johnny's headlight from his bike before dumping it down the embankment, as now he was without. Oh well, too late now. In the movies if you decided to crawl down the hill to grab the spare headlight you would probably injure yourself and end up dying by the bike. He didn't plan on going that way.

As Joe sat there in the dark in front of Hank's stolen pup tent, he realized that he didn't know where Johnny's secret ranch was. He had no way of safely crossing the border and importing all of his coke that he had stashed on his bike. *Fuck it,* Joe thought to himself. *I don't want to be part of this anymore.* It was a bad idea in the first place. In the half-light he proceeded to pull the packed kilos of cocaine out of his saddle bags and toss it over the edge of the hillside. *Good riddance,* Joe thought. *Better off without it.*

After dumping his coke haul Joe felt exhausted. He was still creeped out by the idea of sleeping so close to where his buddy was buried but he was tired enough to lie down in the tent. Within minutes he was asleep. His last thoughts before closing his eyes were that tomorrow, he would be back home. Safe and sound.

CHAPTER FORTY-SIX

Joe woke at dawn. Despite waking up a couple of times in the night due to animals (or something) crawling around his tent he slept fairly well considering the previous day's events. Johnny had killed Hank, Johnny had killed that Dark Legions dude. He had killed Johnny. Self-defense, he kept telling himself. Kill or be killed. He truly believed that if he hadn't shot Johnny, Johnny would have killed him. He had been left with no choice but to kill his friend.

He was hungry and thirsty. Sooner or later, he would need to gas up too. He couldn't afford to run out of gas again. He needed to get going now, head north and rejoin a main road of some form. Now that he wasn't carrying kilos of cocaine on his bike, he felt safe enough to risk riding on the main roads again. It struck him then how paranoid it had made him carrying all that contraband about. Despite the amount of money they would have made if they had succeeded in crossing the border, it just wasn't worth the risks. They should have never been so stupid.

He packed up his meager belongings, checked the paper map again and clambered back on his scoot. Time to get motoring and make it back to Arizona before nightfall. He was glad he still had all his TIPS paperwork, as he was going to be needing that to cross the border the legit way.

As Joe rode the dirt track looking for a side road that would take him north, he contemplated their pursuit of wealth and how it had led to Hank and Johnny's downfall. Paranoia and greed had gotten the best of Johnny. It had eaten him alive. Not good. If Johnny had sold that bike and used the money to pay off his outstanding mortgage payments, he could have found a legal way to keep his head above water. What was the old saying? *"Easy money" schemes are never easy?* They got that right. He had been a fool to go along with his old friend and now for the rest of his life, when he closed his eyes, he would be haunted by Johnny rolling in the Mexican dirt full of bullet holes and dying in agony.

He wouldn't have wished that curse on his worst enemies. *Oh well, what is done is done.* Whatever fate awaited Joe he would deal with when the time came. Would it be quick? Would it be painful? He didn't know, but he did know you can never outrun your karma. Death would come calling sooner or later, and he would have to deal with it when it did.

CHAPTER FORTY-SEVEN

Joe found his way off the dirt road about twenty miles north of his deadly fight with Johnny. He took the 15 north all the way through to Nogales. Crossing the border without contraband made things a lot easier despite the fact he got more grief from the U.S. customs and immigration officers than he did from the Mexicans. He was relieved his paperwork was all in order and finally, they let him pass through. He had done it—he was back in the motherland of his beloved Arizona.

As he rode the familiar roads home, he reflected on his time in Mexico. Despite all the bad things that had happened, he could see himself returning one day, ideally just for a nice legal run, no shenanigans. A lot of great food, stunning architecture, super friendly people and above all, stunning scenery perfect for riding.

He made up his mind then. He would definitely return one day.

Thank You!

Hey this is Alex. If you have made it this far, Thank you!

This is my first novel and I wanted to thank you for taking a chance on me.

If you enjoyed Broken Brotherhood please consider leaving a review as that would greatly help me out.

I've a ton of stories in the pipeline if you want to keep updated on new books head on over to my website : www.alexmcrae.net.

All for now

Alex

Phoenix Arizona 2025

AUTHOR BIOGRAPHY

Alex McRae

Alex McRae has lived all over the world, seen more than his fair share of wild and crazy things, and has the stories to prove it. Lucky to still be alive, he pours his experiences into gripping tales filled with action, grit, and the kind of hard-earned wisdom that only comes from a life well ridden.

A lifelong lover of motorcycles, guns, cold beers, and beautiful women, Alex has been tearing up the open road since the age of 15. These passions fuel his writing, bringing to life the kind of raw, untamed stories that keep readers on the edge of their seats.

Now calling Arizona his adopted home, he thrives in the state's 300 days of sunshine, surrounded by stunning landscapes of rugged deserts and towering mountains. When he's not at his desk crafting his next hard-hitting novel, you can find him out riding, chasing the horizon on two wheels.

Alex McRae writes for those who live fast, ride hard, and believe that every road has a story.

Printed in Dunstable, United Kingdom

70949010R00143